AFTER MIDNIGHT

AFTER MIDNIGHT
True Lesbian Confessions

EDITED BY CHELSEA JAMES

CLEIS
PRESS

Published in the United States by Cleis Press Inc.,
P.O. Box 14697, San Francisco, California 94114.

Printed in the United States.
Cover design: Scott Idleman
Cover photograph: Siege
Text design: Frank Wiedemann
Cleis logo art: Juana Alicia
First Edition.
10 9 8 7 6 5 4 3 2

Diana Cage's "The Sailor" originally appeared in a slightly different form in *Up All Night: Adventures in Lesbian Sex*, edited by Stacy Bias and Rachel Kramer Bussel (Alyson Books, 2004). Kristina Wright's "By Any Other Name" originally appeared in a slightly different form in *Bedroom Eyes: Stories of Lesbians in the Boudoir*, edited by Lesléa Newman (Alyson Books, 2002).

Contents

INTRODUCTION

An intimate encounter in a movie theater halfway across the world. A passionate affair with a married woman. A weekend of role-playing with two women and their "headmistress," Miss Johnson.

The gals in this book tell powerful, raw, sensuous tales ripped from the pages of their sexual lives. In ways they've never before expressed their sultry, playful, and sometimes downright dirty secrets, these women bare all, describing not only their deepest fantasies, but the hot and heavy truth of their sexual deeds inside and outside the bedroom.

Peer in during a young woman's first time getting tag-teamed. Enjoy a rollicking "Toy Story" that's certainly not rated G. Accept a red-hot Valentine's Day gift any horny lesbian would be grateful to receive. In short, curl up—alone or with a lover—and discover what lesbians from around the world are getting up to...after midnight.

Chelsea James

OUR DIRTY LITTLE SECRET

Jenny Dewey

Wednesdays, Club Cruz in North Hollywood became Tryst & Shout. The inside was the same no matter what neon sign outside the old paint factory was lit or what T-shirts the staff wore that night. The music and the videos on the huge screens over the dance floor didn't change from night to night. What made it different was that Wednesdays were our night— drag kings and femmes, bois and gurrls, and lesbians from all over Los Angeles.

Ming-Ye and I went to Tryst & Shout maybe once a month. Dancing in front of people was never easy for me. I played soccer and volleyball, but when the music started, my muscles lost all coordination. Ming-Ye, though, she was born to move. Her arms would slowly rise, her hands reaching for the multicolored lights flashing overhead. Other women watched as the music possessed her. Twirl and bump, and then she'd stop and slyly smile at me as her hips moved in a slow grind. The world would go away and I'd wrap my arms around her. She'd flick back her long black hair and the scent of her soap and shampoo would remind me of being cuddled close to the nape of her neck in bed. Straddling my thigh, she'd move, baby, move, and it was enough that I was there to hold her.

"These boots are killing me," she confessed as we tried to wedge our way through the crowd around the sleek glass bar.

"You say that every time you wear them," I shouted over the pounding music.

Her full lips curled into a wicked grin. "Yeah, but they're hot."

Ming-Ye would have been hot in anything. The year I met her, she was in her "Chinese schoolgirl gone bad" phase. Short plaid skirts, thigh-high stockings, and lipstick the color of plums against skin like warm caramel. Since then, she'd become "librarian gone bad," wearing tailored blouses that cupped her small breasts, her silky hair pulled back in a tight bun, and the ultimate pair of thigh-high black leather spiked heeled boots.

Jostled by the crowd, I had to fight for my balance. I could imagine Ming-Ye rolling her eyes when music turned me into a klutz, but I never caught her at it.

"You want something?" I asked.

"The usual."

At least that's what I thought she said. I couldn't hear her. I nodded and worked my way to the bar, leaving her to stand on the edge of the dance floor.

Sometimes I wondered what she saw in me. We got along well, we laughed a lot, but she turned heads wherever she went. I was okay in a sporty, girl-next-door kind of way. When we went out, I saw the way women looked at her. I knew what they were thinking, because I thought it too. Those lips of Ming-Ye's kissed hard and came away bruised. She looked like the kind of girl who would press a lover against a wall or fuck in an alleyway.

I shuffled forward one step at a time until I reached the edge of the glossy black bar. It was under-lit by fiber-optic strands that changed color in a slow cycle. Blue glow made the bartenders look like the undead. By the time I ordered our drinks, their faces were sickly green with halos reflecting weirdly from their eyes. I was glad to take the drinks and back out of the crush.

A shout rose as the hottest new video showed on the huge screens on the walls around the club. Women surged to the floor, almost sweeping me along.

"Here." I offered Ming-Ye her drink.

She watched the dancers, mesmerized. I tried to guess who she was looking at. She seemed to be staring at a leggy blonde wearing a leather halter top and black jeans.

That woman was a head taller than anyone else in the club, but she was memorable for other reasons. She stood on top of one of the small dance platforms. Her companion, smaller, with dark hair, also shared the tiny stage. Their dance was full-on frottage, the kind of careless sexy moves I wished I could relax enough to enjoy. Watching them felt like peeking through someone's window, though. I was a little ashamed that it turned me on so much.

The blonde had a great body and excellent hair. A perfect California beach volleyball goddess, she was one of those women everyone claims to hate on sight but secretly wants to meet.

Damn it, she could really dance too. Just Ming-Ye's type.

I elbowed Ming-Ye. "Your drink."

"Thanks." She didn't even bother to glance at me. Her big brown eyes stayed fixed on the woman even as she took a sip.

That pissed me off. I didn't think of myself as the type that got jealous, but Ming-Ye couldn't tear her eyes from the blonde long enough to even acknowledge that I was there. Mean words welled up in my throat, nearly choking me. Surprised at myself, I looked everywhere except at Ming-Ye so that she wouldn't catch me being an idiot.

Someone bumped into me. I moved a few steps. The next bump seemed more deliberate, so I spun around, ready to make a nasty comment, when I realized my teammate from the women's soccer league was standing there.

"Jen!" Carrie grinned.

"Hey. Didn't expect to see you here."

Oh, man, did she see me staring dagger eyes at the blonde on top of the platform?

We chatted a bit about our team and our last game, but we weren't really friends, so that was all we had to talk about. Pretty soon, we were down to, "This DJ has the best mixes," and "So, how far away did you have to park?" It got more awkward by the minute, and the pauses grew longer, so I decided to put us both out of our misery.

"Well, it was great seeing you, but I'm here with someone."

"Yeah, right." She grinned again and bobbed her head, probably grateful she could move on. "Catch you later."

I looked around for Ming-Ye but didn't see her. She was probably out on the dance floor, or she'd met someone she knew. We weren't clingy. We had separate friends, and we ran into many of them at Tryst & Shout.

After circling the club four times in search of her, I was pretty steamed. She was nowhere to be seen. And then it hit me—I hadn't seen that blonde anywhere either.

Ming-Ye had dumped me.

I had no idea where that idea came from, but as soon as the poison was in my heart, I couldn't ignore it.

My eyes stung. The crowd was too close and the music pounded against my ribs. I needed room. I wanted to breathe air that wasn't thick with the sharp scent of girl sweat. The lights were too hot, and misery filled my belly.

No. She wouldn't dump me. Ming-Ye *never* looked at other women.

Not that I knew of, the voice of doubt whispered in my ear. I hadn't caught her at it. That didn't mean anything.

Get a grip, I told myself.

I got out my cell phone and pushed the speed dial for Ming-Ye. Her voice mail picked up. Swearing, I stalked through the crowd again.

My last circuit brought me to the back of the club. A long line for the women's room snaked back almost to the bar. I was angry enough that I planned to leave with or without Ming-Ye.

First, though, before the long ride home, a pit stop.

Ming-Ye and I shared a little secret. We had figured out months back that although men were allowed into the club, few came on Wednesdays. It wasn't like the rest of the week when the crowd was mostly gay, with a fair amount of lesbians and a few straights to round out the mix. So while everyone else stood obediently in line for the women's room, Ming-Ye and I always sneaked into the men's room. Five stalls, no waiting. The one time we walked in on a guy, he grinned at us.

I went to the men's room door. Being cautious, I cracked it open and glanced in. No one stood at the urinals along the wall, so I figured it was safe. A couple steps in, though, I realized I wasn't alone. A little groan gave someone away. I saw feet under one of the stall doors.

Black jeans.

The ceiling in the men's room was mirrored, even over the stalls. I'd heard stories about how our gay friends watched guys giving blow jobs, and how hot it was to watch. I envied the way they could be so open about it.

I glanced up and saw blonde hair. The woman was standing in an odd position, sort of bending down. Someone else was in there with her. Under the black metal door, I saw impossibly high heels, and a pair of familiar black boots.

I almost ripped off the door right then. Looking back up to the ceiling, I tried to see for sure if Ming-Ye was in there, but the boots were enough proof. I froze. I didn't want to see it. I didn't want to know. And yet, I had to.

My heart pounded so hard I could feel the beat behind my eyes. Fear and disbelief squeezed my lungs.

I heard another groan.

The men's room smelled like men, but I caught a whiff of pure female scent cutting through it. Music thumped against the door. A slick, wet sound could barely be heard above it.

I was sick. I wanted to cry, but something about that sound and the smell of sex sent tight tingles shooting through me. Ming-Ye was cheating on me. I should have hauled her cheating whore ass out of there and told her to go to hell, but instead I tiptoed into the stall next to them.

With my ear pressed against the cold metal partition, I could hear the rustle of skirt being hiked up. Above me, the mirror showed the blonde unbuttoning a red shirt, pushing up a bra, teasing a pale brown nipple with her fingers.

The cheaters murmured. Then their lips mashed together. I held my breath as long as they kissed. We all panted when they separated for a moment. They lunged together again.

It was so wrong to look, but Ming-Ye was my lover. Didn't I have the right to watch her? Or maybe we were over and I was the only one who didn't know it. I never saw it coming.

Fuck it. I'd watch.

The snap of panties being pulled aside was hard to hear over the slam of fingers against a wet clit.

They banged against the stall, forgetting to be quiet.

She wasn't like that, I thought. Ming-Ye wasn't passive. She'd never lean against a wall, teetering on those ridiculous heels with her legs spread while she waited for another woman to make all the moves. Ming-Ye grabbed what she wanted and took it hard.

The blonde's hand worked in obvious circles.

I imagined Ming-Ye's clit getting fat under the stroke of a thumb.

Shocked, I realized that I was turned on. My body was confused, I decided. Adrenaline made me feel amped and unreal, as if I couldn't really be seeing what I thought I was.

The twinges in my clit got harder to ignore. I felt the weight of a drop of cum hanging, waiting to fall, ready to be lapped up by Ming-Ye's tongue. It seemed to magnify the sensations of every nerve.

My hand slid down into my underwear.

The slightest touch sent shock waves of excitement through my body. My hand pulled my outer lips tight against my clit, squeezing it as my other hand rubbed quick and harsh.

Did Ming-Ye's new lover tug at her sex, pulling it like taffy until Ming-Ye gasped, "Too much"? It seemed weird that Ming-Ye didn't have the blonde on her knees. I felt as if I didn't know her at all.

Leaning against the far wall of the stall, I put my foot up on the toilet and braced myself as my hand worked in harder, faster strokes.

I listened to the lovers' little gasps of pleasure and watched them in the overhead mirror as I avoided looking at my own reflection.

Was Ming-Ye getting a finger up inside her, like I was? Did two, and then three, fingers fuck her while her thumb stroked circles over the sensitive nub? Were her lover's fingers drenched in juices like mine were? I hoped not, but the moans in the stall next to me got deeper.

She never moaned like that for me. She was always so quiet while her lips flushed deep pink and her eyes closed. Sometimes, only a tremor running through her body, and the gush of sweet flavor let me know she'd come.

"Yes, yes," a voice in the next stall said.

Yes, yes, I was almost there too. Release was riding a tense wave that could crash at any moment over my body.

"Fuck me," someone said in an awed whisper. It was clearly Ming-Ye's voice bouncing off the tiled walls of the bathroom.

Startled, her blonde lover pulled back, but then she shrugged and I heard the moans again.

Yes, fuck her, I thought. Fuck Ming-Ye. We were so fucking over.

I was mad at myself for being so turned on, but I couldn't help it. I couldn't walk away, couldn't even think, until I'd come.

I rubbed harder, working myself up into a froth of anger and sex. My nipples, hardened by desire, rubbed against the inside of my bra.

The stall walls banged in fuck rhythm as the blonde and the cheater whore slammed against it.

Heat rushed across my face. I could hear my pulse thudding in my ears and feel it in my clit. I looked up, hoping the sight of the lovers in the next stall would send me over the edge.

I stood up on my toes. It was unexpected, the harsh jolt of intense orgasm that ripped through me. Fast, throbbing, it knocked me back against the toilet. I held onto the wall, panting.

The girl in the next stall over hit her orgasm hard too.

"God," she gulped. "God…"

Since when did Ming-Ye talk about God?

When I made her come, she danced on the tip of my tongue. Fingers grasping my hair, she'd pull me into her and grind, baby, grind to sultry music only she heard. Her butt would lift up and growling, she'd shimmy. Then, grinning, she'd collapse back on the couch, legs spread.

At least she didn't dance for the blonde. She sort of just stood there and let it happen.

Good. Let the blonde think she was a half-assed fuck, one of those girls who didn't lose their minds for sex, no matter how awesome.

I watched the blonde bring her fingers to her nose, watched her sniff, watched her smile. I was going to kill her.

And then, in the reflection overhead, I saw another pair of eyes, glinting with suppressed laughter.

Startled, guilty, I looked away, and then up at the reflection again. In the stall on the far side, Ming-Ye was hunched over, alone. Her merry gaze met mine and as her shoulders shook from suppressed laughter, she put a finger to her lips, urging me to stay quiet. Her other hand, the one I couldn't see, I somehow knew worked over her clit.

It wasn't her with the blonde. It was all just a mistake.

Ming-Ye's eyes half closed in that way I knew so well. Her mouth opened in a perfect little O of pleasure. Quietly, she shuddered through her climax. After she had pushed her skirt down, she blew me a kiss from a hand that I knew was coated with her juices. She winked at me.

Ashamed at myself for doubting Ming-Ye, I blushed and bowed my head.

The other couple pulled their clothes back on and stole out of the men's room.

I heard footsteps. Ming-Ye knocked on the stall door. I

couldn't hide forever, so I finally opened it. She wasn't pissed. She grinned at me. She had no idea what I'd been thinking.

She extended her hand, and I took it even though I didn't deserve to.

"Oh, honey," she told me as she kissed me. "Don't be embarrassed. I've always gotten off on watching. It's okay."

I almost cried. How could she be nice to me?

"Did you see that bitch wearing my boots? I couldn't believe it when I saw her on the dance floor."

Something between laughter and a sob shook me. I should have known it was the boots. I never even looked at the blonde's lover.

Ming-Ye caressed my face with her petite hands. "So you get off on watching too? I never guessed. Maybe you have a wild streak after all. But don't worry. I won't tell anyone. This'll be our dirty little secret."

A FUCKING GOOD TIME

Mary Deveraux

Julie and I had been best friends for a long time. We were on vacation together and had just come back from a day at the beach. We sat relaxing on our hotel-room balcony looking down at all the bodies lying on the sand.

We were discussing lesbians.

"Oh, come on now, Mary," she said. "You're not trying to tell me you've never even thought about it."

"I haven't," I told her, and took a sip of my drink.

"Never?"

I shook my head.

"You're lying," she persisted.

"I'm not." I downed my drink. My cheeks were flushed not only from the liquor but from the drilling Julie was giving me.

"You're trying to tell me that not once during the whole time you were married, you and John never, ever talked about it?"

"Nope."

"Never fantasized about a woman going down on you? Ever?"

"Er...well...um..."

"Yeah, that's what I thought," she laughed.

The alcohol gave me the courage I needed. I was dying to tell her what I really wanted, so I thought, *Why not?* I could always blame the drinking if things went wrong.

"To tell you the truth..." I began hesitantly.

"Yeah! What?" Julie urged.

"I've always been kind of attracted to you," I practically whispered.

"Oh, have you now? And what have you fantasized about?" She opened and closed her legs, giving me glimpses of the crotch of her panties.

I licked my lips, hoping I looked seductive enough. I knew how to flirt with guys but wasn't sure what would turn on a woman.

"I've wondered what it would be like being naked in front of you," I told her. "To have you touch and caress me." I couldn't believe I'd actually said it.

"There's only one way to find out." She rose from her lounge chair and helped me stand up. She removed my bikini right there on the balcony where anyone could see us. "Is this how you thought it would be?" she said. "Standing naked before me with my fingers brushing against your breasts?"

"Oh, yes." I giggled nervously as my nipples hardened under her stroking.

"Do you like me touching you? Does it make you feel hot and tingly when I touch you here? And what about there?"

Her hands moved from my breasts, over my hips, to my ass, which she grabbed, squeezing the cheeks as she pulled me gently toward her, her finger slipping into my crack to linger lightly on my hole.

"Oh, yes. That feels so good," I told her, my pussy throbbing.

Julie's hands were all over me now. As they slipped over my mound and into my slit, my legs went weak and my knees buckled. She pushed me back into my lounge chair and stood in front of me as she slowly peeled off her bikini.

Her body was magnificent—her breasts full, her nipples dark, begging to be sucked. She had no hair at all on her pussy, and I couldn't tear my eyes away from her slit. Her lips protruded slightly, glistening wet with desire.

She was so at ease with her body, and I envied that, the way she braced herself against the railing, not caring if anyone saw her. She turned to face the beach, giving anyone who might have been looking a bird's-eye view of her naked body in all its glory. Her sweet ass was right in front of me, begging for me to fondle it.

Turning back, Julie smiled as she knelt beside me to run her hands over my perky breasts, pinching my rigid nipples before moving down my stomach to my hairy mound, where she roughly knocked my knees apart so she could inspect me.

I watched as her fingers probed my lips, sliding in and out of the folds, fiddling with the rings I'd had pierced there. She hooked them into her fingers and gently pulled. My pussy gaped open and her nose sniffed delicately.

"Hmm, that's one gorgeous pussy you've got there," she said, staring hard at me.

I didn't know what to say, so I just lay there with my legs open, the sun beating down on my naked pussy, warming me up—as if I wasn't already hot enough—and my juices began to flow.

"Can I lick you? Can I taste you?" she asked.

"Yes," I breathed, dying to have her mouth on me.

"Oh, mmm," she mumbled into my pussy. "You taste *sooooo* good."

She pulled back, taking in my reaction, then ran her hands up over my tits, squeezing them together before continuing her licking. I watched as her tongue, wet with saliva, lavished me with caresses. Her nose brushed against my clit while she tweaked my nipples between her fingers.

"Oh, God. That's beautiful," I moaned. "Just beautiful."

"Look at how hard your nipples are. You like this, don't you?"

"Oh, yes. Squeeze them harder. Oh, yeah. Like that. Mmm. Harder."

"Like this?"

"Oh, fuck. Yes." I arched my back and thrust my breasts toward her as my body convulsed, an orgasm threatening to explode from me.

"You fucking horny bitch," Julie said, as her fingers pushed their way inside my saturated pussy and her mouth latched onto my breast.

"Oh, that feels good…. Bite down. Harder. Oh, yeah, I like that. That's fucking fabulous." I pushed my pelvis into her hand as she slammed in and out of me.

Never in my wildest dreams had I thought it would be this good. My clit throbbed like mad as she sucked and bit my nipple. I held her head firmly, my thighs clenching. Shaking uncontrollably, I kept her there as an orgasm rippled through me.

I was desperate now. I had to touch her, taste her, feel her—all of her—so I pulled her head up toward me. She withdrew her fingers, which dripped with my juices. She climbed up my body until her mouth was directly over mine, our breasts touching, our pelvises grinding against each other. She lowered her head to kiss me, my wetness smeared all over her face, the taste of me thick on her lips.

Her kiss had me reeling. Weak, I pushed her away from me, grabbing at her tits, my chest rising and falling as I breathed heavily. With my juices running down the inside of my thighs, I grabbed her, dragged her inside the room, and threw her on the bed.

Her legs opened, and I fell between them, enjoying my first taste of another woman. My head spun as I licked her hard, my tongue lapping at her, licking her clit, probing under the hood then flickering over her clit again. I pulled her into me, breathing in her scent, before my hands roamed upward to knead those luscious breasts.

"Oh, yeah. Squeeze my nipples," she said. "I love it. Oh, yeah. Your tongue...that's great, just great." Her knees tightened, holding me securely.

"Like that?" I whispered, wanting reassurance.

"That's perfect. Just perfect."

Her hairless pussy tasted fantastic. I lapped at her lips, my tongue slipping in and out of the folds. With my tongue flat, I licked her hole then delved between the folds to find her clit, which I sucked into my mouth. I pulled her lips apart, pushed my fingers deep inside her, the warmth and scent of her pussy intoxicating me.

"I love it... You taste so good," I said as I pulled back, my face wet with her hot juices.

"Kiss me," Julie begged. "I want to taste myself in your mouth."

"I can't get enough of you," I told her, grabbing her tits and nipping the flesh with quick bites.

I kissed her hard, my tongue searching out hers, but I wanted more.

I turned her over and showered her with kisses, working my way down her spine until I came to the cleft of her asscheeks. I ran my tongue over her hole and licked lazily over it. I hunkered down, pulling apart her cheeks and enjoying the feel of her puckered skin before inching in a finger.

"Oh, yes," Julie sighed.

She pushed back into my face, obviously enjoying what I was doing. I lay on her back, my hard nipples poking into her, while I thrust my pelvis forward, imitating a cock, riding my pussy over her gorgeous ass.

Wiggling out of my grasp, she rolled over and pulled me toward her. We wrestled together, laughing as we grappled at each other before she assumed a sixty-nine position over me.

"Oh, that's feels great," I said. "Bring your pussy down on me...further...quickly. Come on, stop teasing me.... Bring that hairless cunt to me."

She laughed as she lowered herself over me, and we nuzzled into each other, licking, sucking, and exploring. My fingers dug deep into her soft flesh then plunged inside to finger her. Her juices oozed out to mingle with my saliva before I rubbed her hardened nub madly and brought her to an earth-shattering orgasm.

"Oh, God!" she screamed. "That's so fucking good. Are you sure you've never done this before?"

"Never," I laughed. "But I'll be doing more of it in future. Fuck, I love your cunt."

I adore the word *cunt*. So raw, so powerful. As I dipped my fingers back inside her I wondered *why* I'd never done this before. It was fucking amazing.

"Finger me deeper," Julie said. "Deeper, deeper. Harder, yeah. Fuck me harder...harder. Oh, yeah."

"You're so fucking hot and wet," I told her. "So fucking horny."

"Oh, yeah, baby. Harder...harder...I'm coming..."

I went wild, finger-fucking her like crazy, my fingers swimming inside her soaked cunt as she ate me out.

"Quick. Rub my clit," she said. "Yeah…more. Keep going."

"Fuck. Faster. Faster…"

"Rub harder," she said. "Oh, fuck, yeah. Like that. Don't stop. Please don't stop. I'm coming…I'm coming…"

"I'm coming too," I moaned. "Faster…right there. Keep going…keep going…"

"I'm coming…coming… Oh, God yes…"

We lay there together until Julie slipped from the bed. Confused, I called out to her and she came back wearing a dildo. I spread my legs hungrily, eager for a good fucking.

"When we're finished here," she said, "we're getting dressed to the nines, and tonight we're bringing back some women."

"What?" I laughed.

"Come on now, someone as horny as you? Don't tell me you've never fantasized about a foursome."

"Threesome, foursome, orgy—what's the difference?" I said. "When I'm with you I want it all."

She lay on her back, the dildo pointing skyward. I impaled myself on it and watched her gorgeous face light up as I slid up and down the shaft. Coming here with Julie had taken our relationship to an entirely new level.

I knew we were going to have a good time, a real fucking good time.

CONTROL
FREAK

Tanya Turner

I didn't know quite how much of a control freak my friend Cindy was until we had a threesome. That's when her true nature made itself known. And by that point I was naked and more than willing to cater to her whims. But I'm getting ahead of myself. Cindy and I had been friends for a few years, meeting at professional conferences and conversing via email. When she told me she was moving to New York to live with a woman she'd met online, I was thrilled, and we proceeded to paint the town red, sometimes with her girlfriend Emma, sometimes on our own. Plenty of our booze-soaked nights ended with our making out on some couch in the corner of a dive bar, or her coming home with me and our falling on top of each other; having lusty, drunken, sloppy sex, and waking up in the morning with our hair plastered every which way, our throats dry and our bodies sore. Emma was more of a stay-at-home kind of girl, but she didn't mind our carousing. Until that fateful night, everything was separated by neat dividing lines. I'd eat calm, adult sushi dinners with the two of them, and have long, rambling conversations over Sapporo and spicy tuna, with barely a hint of sexual tension in the room.

But one afternoon, Cindy asked me if I'd consider having a threesome with them. "Almost every night we've been talking about bringing someone else into our bed," she said. "Emma wants to watch me with another girl, and well, you're the most likely candidate. In fact—well, don't get upset—but I sometimes tell her about what we do together, and it makes her so wet, you wouldn't believe it."

"Really?" I raised my eyebrows. "Quiet little Emma, with the sweaters and pearls? Who drinks her tea and is so polite all the time?"

"Believe me, Tanya. In bed she's nothing like she is when you've seen her. The only thing is, well, she wants to watch us, and she and I might fool around, but I don't want you two having sex."

I got the feeling Cindy was afraid that Emma, or I, might like it just a little too much. I didn't really see how we could have a proper threesome when two of the three people involved weren't supposed to so much as make out, but my curiosity got the better of me. Most of my escapades with Cindy had been almost afterthoughts, fueled as much by boredom and alcohol as anything else. It wasn't like we were so ravenous we couldn't keep our hands off each other. But maybe that was only because I'd considered her taken. Plus, we'd been friends for so long. Even so, my mind churned with the possibilities, my pussy throbbing almost despite myself.

"Okay," I told her. "I'm in. What's the plan?" Cindy's the kind of girl who *always* has a plan.

"How about Saturday night? Our place. Eight o'clock. Wear

something sexy," she said, her fuchsia lips only slightly lighter than her magenta bob, both offset by her super-pale skin. Her cool brown eyes stared into mine with their laser-beam focus, and I couldn't have said no even if I'd wanted to. With her unique fashion choices, Cindy could never have gotten a job in corporate America, but she has a way of getting what she wants that rivals any CEO, male or female, around.

I spent the next three days hunting for the perfect outfit. All my lingerie seemed dated, over the top, or boring. I needed something new, special. I went to my favorite local shop, my nose quivering as I stepped into the overly scented boutique, my nostrils immediately invaded by the ticklish feather boas lining the walls. I zoomed in on an old-fashioned-looking one-piece, a baby-blue and black lace slip, sheer and gauzy, really just a wisp of fabric. It had matching panties, not a tedious thong but something real and sexy that would actually cover and cling to my ass, drawing attention to it with every move. Part of me knew it was silly to blow a quarter of my paycheck on something that would likely only stay on me for a brief time, but I needed it to get me in the mood. As intrigued as I was by the idea of getting to know the mysterious Emma a little better, I was a little unnerved by Cindy's take-charge attitude. I was used to it one-on-one, liked it even, but how would that play out with the three of us involved?

I made the purchase, tucking the new lingerie away with a little potpourri-scented satchet until the big night. I barely ate anything all day, picking at my bowl of cereal, swigging tea and finally a glass of wine before I donned my delicates. Over the undies and slip, I wore a simple dress and my signature fishnets, along with spiky heels, grateful Cindy and Emma only lived two blocks away. I spritzed my cleavage, neck, and wrists with my favorite scent, and I was off. When I arrived, their cozy one-bedroom apartment was filled with candles.

Cindy greeted me with a lusty kiss, pinning me to the door as she slid one leg, barely covered by her vinyl miniskirt, between my legs. She pressed her knee against my crotch, moving much faster than I'd have expected. I let her kiss me for a minute then pushed her away, not sure what was about to happen. I'd shown up for a threesome, but suddenly I was unsure. I scanned the room for Emma and spotted her in one corner. She had a slightly nervous look on her face, just like I did. I smiled at her, taking in her sweet little white cardigan with a strand of pearl beads, the lacy white tank top underneath, and her long, simple black skirt that wrapped around her tiny body.

I swilled the beer Cindy handed me and let the cold, soothing liquid fill me with courage. Not that I needed it, particularly, but these situations can be nerve-wracking. But then Cindy moved in to save the day, summoning Emma and me to the couch and planting herself between us. She turned to kiss Emma, pressing her wet, beery lips up against her girlfriend's, teasing her with quick darts of her tongue, before she turned back to me. When she sucked on my lower lip, I moaned, and her hand went to my nipples. I took a peek at Emma to see if she looked uncomfortable, but she didn't seem to mind.

Cindy placed her beer on the floor, then returned to my breasts and twisted both nipples as Emma took off her sweater. She had what my friends and I call "secret boobs"—the kind that look fairly average until a girl unveils them to reveal herself as the next incarnation of Dolly Parton. Wow! I was in awe, especially since her cardigan and every other shirt she owned had managed to keep these amazing tatas hidden. I longed to touch them and play with them, much like Cindy was doing to me, but I couldn't. I'd promised Cindy she would be the center of attention. So instead I pushed her down, making her tumble on top of Emma. I placed my hand on her inner thigh, then lightly brushed it against her panties. Both girls were lying on their backs, Cindy pressing against Emma, her head cushioned by ample breasts. I wanted to touch both of them at once—after all, there were three of us—but when my hand dipped from Cindy's thigh to Emma's, Cindy reached down and quick as a flash set me straight.

"You can only touch me, remember?" she said, and I resigned myself to having one pretty girl to play with—not a bad deal, really. I eased off her panties and pushed up her skirt while Emma played with Cindy's nipples. Our ringleader let out delighted squeals as I pushed my head between her legs and ate her out, my tongue cold with the latest sip from my chilly beer bottle. I licked and lapped and sucked and feasted on her responsive pussy while she gyrated her hips, pushing against me until she finally came, trembling between us.

I crawled on top of Cindy, the three of us forming one big pile. Cindy and I kissed while my fingers lazily trailed up and down her arm. Then she slipped her leg between mine, pressing against my own moistness, and we almost fell off the couch. She sat up, and it was her turn to push me down. She lifted first my dress, then my slip, revealing my recent purchase, which was now totally wet with my juices.

Cindy peeled down my panties and dipped her fingers lower to stroke my wetness, and I let out a fierce cry, pushing back against her to try to get her inside me. But apparently she had other plans. "Emma, put your finger in Tanya's ass," she said. I was shocked at this turn of events! I thought Emma and I were supposed to stay away from each other, but I wasn't going to argue.

I heard muffled whispers while I waited patiently for someone—by that point, my body on the verge of exploding, I didn't care who—to touch me. I peeked behind me when I felt soft, warm fingers stroke my ass. Emma's hands were small, but they felt incredible. She wasn't as fast and fierce as Cindy, but it was a nice change of pace.

Cindy got up from the couch and sat on the floor near us, watching. Then Emma did something I completely didn't expect: She leaned down, and with her small pink tongue she licked my asshole. Her tongue darted along my puckered flesh, and I felt my panties bunch against me as her mouth made me wetter and wetter. She kept tickling and tormenting me, tapping against my back hole with her tongue until finally she pressed her finger against the wet opening. I let her in right away, and she eased that lone finger slowly between my cheeks. I gripped her tight, clutching her and drawing her deeper into my ass, while her other hand finally stroked my pussy.

Emma didn't even wait for Cindy's permission. She just deftly began working my cunt, her fingers curling and pressing and curving and stretching as the fingers of her other hand pushed deeper into my tight tunnel. Little Emma with the big boobs was proving herself to be one talented dyke. She knew exactly when to touch me, exactly when to press harder and when to pull back, where to stroke and how to bring me tantalizingly close to orgasm before retreating. She was a careful lover, deliberate and economical with her touches. She was focused on one thing and one thing only—my pleasure. Perhaps that's why Cindy had changed her mind, or maybe she'd planned this all along.

As Emma continued to plumb both of my tender holes, I looked at Cindy, who grinned at us with delight. Maybe she'd planned it all along. She's such a control freak about everything else—I'm sure it's hard for her to leave her inner planner at the bedroom—or in this case, living room—door. But I wasn't angry. How could I be when Emma was thrusting into me, using her short fingers to full advantage, fucking me with four of them in my pussy? I could barely move as her efforts wrung out every drop of my resistance, along with plenty of my juices. When Emma added her thumb, tucking it in and nudging my slick opening, I cried out, tears filling my eyes. I had lost control completely, giving myself over to this girl whose body and talents I'd never really thought much about.

When Emma had gotten her whole hand inside me, she paused, giving encouraging coos as she moved infinitesimally, letting my body come to its own conclusions. I felt myself contract, restrict, pulled as if by gravity to the center of my body, then released like a comet, exploding outward, high above us. We'd moved past the carefree, lighthearted stage of the evening into a space where none of us had control.

When Emma finally extricated herself from me, I buried my head in the couch. I didn't know what to say. I wasn't embarrassed so much as stunned at how deep she'd taken me when we hadn't even kissed, let alone really talked. Maybe we didn't need to in order to go to those deep, dark, mysterious places. Or maybe we just needed someone like Cindy, bless her heart, to guide us.

NOW IT'S MY TURN

Aine Ni Cheallaigh

Here's something you should know about my girlfriend: She's obsessed with equality. She's a Libra. The scales must always balance. It's Sunday afternoon, and she's going to her mother's. Before she leaves, she makes it a point to remind me that it's my turn.

"Please make sure you do all the dishes."

"Yup." I'm lying on the couch in an old stained T-shirt, watching TV.

"Are you listening?"

I tear my eyes from the screen and look at her attentively.

"It's not fair," she says. "I always do a very thorough cleaning job and I would like to see you do the same. For once."

Here's the thing you should know about me: I'm a procrastinator. My motto is, "Why do something today when you can put it off and end up not doing it at all?" So after she leaves, I stay on the couch like I'm glued to it, one eye on the clock, knowing I should start. But come on, cleaning sucks, right? I keep telling myself, *Five more minutes.*

Then those five minutes are up and I think, *Okay, just five more minutes.*

This could end badly.

Then bingo! I get an idea. I remember the time we read Betty Dodson's *Sex for One* out loud to each other. We alternated chapters, of course, to keep it even. I remember a story about a woman, this housewife, who would clean for an hour then lie down for five minutes to tease herself with her vibrator, then get up for another hour with five minutes of fun waiting at the end.

I think, *I'm there!*

I'm up and running, my mind racing. We don't have a big apartment to clean, so I perform some quick modifications on the concept. I know it'll work. I'm a genius!

Here are my rules:

1. I have to keep upright, no lying down.

2. I have to keep cleaning without stopping for any significant amount of time.

3. But while I'm cleaning, I can get off any way I want.

And then I throw in a curve ball:

4. The blinds have to stay open.

I start with the dishes. There are a lot of them. I'm gonna be here for a while, standing in front of the sink. Pulling out a greasy pan, I start with a dirty fantasy: I picture that woman in Dodson's book putting in a load of laundry then kneeling over her Hitachi Magic Wand, teasing her cunt a little, then pulling back, then teasing again. It's getting me going.

Reaching to the windowsill for the steel wool, I feel my hip brush against something hard. It's the handle on the fake drawer that fronts the sink. I scrub and scrub and oh-so-casually wiggle down to see if I can get the little gold knob into a position I can use. Oh, yes. If I stand in close, it pushes neatly against my clit. God bless our landlord for the thoughtful renovation he did on our kitchen. The next fifteen minutes of dishes fly by. I quickly wipe down the counters and turn to the stove. Lots of baked-on crud there. I scrub and scrub and check out the action on the knobs on the stove: right height but a bit pointy. And I'm also afraid I'll make a wrong move and accidentally set myself on fire. Not a pretty picture. I move on.

The living room is full of possibilities. I have little moments as I lean up against the table edge while I polish it, or straddle the arm of the sofa while I plump up the cushions. But if I really have to keep cleaning without stopping, I can't linger in these delights. I miss my friend, the gold knob in the kitchen. We got so much work done together.

There has to be a way. Then, holding the can of Pledge between my legs for a moment while I dust, I have an idea. I go to the closet in the bedroom. The one with the sex-toy box. The door opens at an angle that hides what I'm doing. That's right, nosy lady across the street, I'm just getting some cleaning supplies. I dig around until I come up with the prize: the lavender dildo my girlfriend and I bought last week at Babeland. I slip it into my underwear with the flared base lying against my clit, while the curved head dips into my wetness. And, boy, am I wet.

On to the bathroom. I squat, I lean, I lunge, I reach. Every turn exerts a new pressure in my pussy, every angle another sweet sensation. Then the bedroom. While I'm squirming across the bed to tuck in the far corner of the sheet, the dildo shifts and slides all the way inside. I moan and rock a little to anchor it inside more firmly. Standing up, I take a few experimental steps to see if it'll slide out. It stays put, and I hang up the laundry enjoying the satisfying feeling of fullness.

I'm in the homestretch now. Just the vacuuming to go. But my clit is crying out for something to rub against, and I don't want to pull out the dildo. Before I start the vacuum cleaner, I stop at the sex-toy box. I pull out an egg-shaped vibrator and slip it into my panties. The remote control goes into my pocket. I don't turn it on. Not yet.

Ah, vacuuming, a one-handed job. My free hand strays into my pocket and flicks on the switch, just for a few seconds. I like the buzz, so I give myself another hit. Halfway through the living room, I decide to leave the vibrator on at low buzz. By the time I get to the bedroom, it's on high and every step I take pushes me closer to the brink. Just the study to go.

I don't want to turn the vibrator down, so while I thrust the vacuum under the desk, I think of cold showers and ice, like some kind of football jock who can't keep his little man down. That does it. I drop the vacuum and straddle my girlfriend's office chair. I imagine I'm a golden boy-hunk of muscle, giving it to her, fucking her deep with my great big dick. I arch my back and come hard and long. The blood rushes to my head, and I see black spots in front of my eyes. They clear up, but the rushing in my ears won't go away. Then I realize it's the vacuum I've left running.

I peel myself off the chair and pick up the vacuum. I spot a dust bunny in the corner and aim for it. But the fantasy isn't letting go. In my fantasy, my girlfriend, who I've just nailed, pulls me from behind. I drop the vacuum and let her push me to the floor. "Where do you think you're going, big boy?" she says, lifting her little cheerleader skirt. She straddles me and grinds her wetness on my belly, then leans down and whispers in my ear. "We're not done yet," she says. " 'Cause now it's my turn."

PAGES FOR YOU

Twana Goodman

Digging through the stack of magazines by my girlfriend Larissa's bed (mostly *Ebony* and *Sports Illustrated*, with some *Vanity Fair*s and a few motorcycle magazines thrown in for good measure), I find a copy of *Hustler*. It's two years old and the cover's a little creased, but the women look the same as if their photos were printed today. Their bodies are glistening with oil, or maybe sweat. Their breasts jut straight out, varnished and hard. Their tiny tufts of pubic hair point the way to carnation-pink insides, tinted in Photoshop by an art assistant who probably pinkens hundreds of pussies a month.

There'd be no reason for Larissa to hide the magazine from me. She knows I love porn, the skankier the better. I'm sure it was just absentmindedly shoved toward the bottom of the pile. Still, I've never seen a magazine like this one in her house. As far as I know, she never buys the stuff, not even *Playboy*. In fact, she claims to hate straight porn. Can't stomach all that cock, or the long-nailed skinny white girls. When I talk about images that get me hot—women tied up, submissive, debased, begging for it—she reminds me that she has feminist sensibilities, and the look she gives me embarrasses both me and my libido.

I wonder if Larissa jerks off while looking at these pictures. Suddenly I realize that in the year we've been together, I've never once seen her masturbate. I've prodded myself with every toy she owns, as well as a few juicy-looking kitchen implements. Pranced around her house naked, save for a butt plug in my ass and clamps on my nipples. All for her enjoyment. Her titillation. But she has never once reciprocated. "I'm a voyeur," she tells me.

How does Larissa do it? Does she use a vibrator? Does she even take off her pants? I imagine her thick fingers parting her bush, finding her hard clit. The fingers at the end of her well-muscled, cocoa-brown arms. The same fingers that feel so good burrowing deep down in my cunt. The fingers she uses to tease my pussy open before her fist—jammed against my cervix—reduces me to a panting, mewing, begging hole. Those fingers. My lover's fingers.

"Small hard circles," she tells me when I touch her. As if I would try anything else. I love it when she tenses up, her clit a hard knot beneath my tongue; her fist clutching a handful of my hair, shoving my face into her wetness until I can't breathe. She holds me there, and I take a big breath before she starts in on me, because there will be no more air for me until she finishes.

The thought of her looking at these dirty pictures, jeans pushed down, fingers dipping into her drenched, salty cunt; making circles, furtively putting in a digit or two, then banging herself silly—oh, God, it makes me wet. I clench my thighs and concentrate on the heat in my crotch as I turn the pages. I wonder which spread does it for her the most. I bet it's the voluptuous black chick with the huge breasts getting the all-anal action. Yeah, that's the one all right.

The image is too much to bear, and my throbbing clit demands attention. I push up my skirt, *Hustler* girls forgotten. In my mind, Larissa is on her back. Her jeans and jockey shorts are bunched around her boots. Her smooth skin is clammy, and she's breathing hard. Her work shirt is open, and she's wearing clamps on her small, hard nipples. Her closely shorn hair is damp with sweat. She's jamming two fingers into her pussy and rubbing her clit at the same time. Her face is red, and all her muscles are tensed. She swears under her breath, "Fuck, fuck, fuck, fuck…" as her fingers push her closer to orgasm. She groans and it sounds like a growl.

Oh, baby, let yourself go, I think. *Let it come.* I push my panties to the side and softly touch my pussy. I'm slick with excitement. My fingers move quickly and lightly over my lips, spreading my wetness. My clit is a hard button, a marble. I roll it between my fingers. The excitement climbs up my cunt into my breasts and arms and hands. I'm on fire. Everything—pussy, ass, clit, fingers—is entwined in a burning knot of tight heat.

I lean back into the pillows and go to town on my aching clit. In my fantasy, Larissa is breathing hard. She's moaning loudly. I flip her over. She's on her knees taking it like a gay boy from some unseen top. She's yelling her head off, bucking against a hard cock, demanding it: *harder, faster, more.* In real life, Larissa comes quietly. She grunts softly and jerks her body off the bed. I'm the screamer. Sometimes she fucks me so hard that I'm hoarse the next day.

I come with a mixture of pleasure and guilt. Panties back in place, skirt down, the blush on my chest and neck begins to fade. Does Larissa know what I just did to her? Should I mention that I found her secret stash? I humbly close the magazine and stick it back into the middle of the pile, right where it was before, nestled snugly between Johnny Depp and Michael Jordan.

MY HELPFUL SECRETARY

Veronica Jones

Stretching back in my chair I looked over to the full-length window of my office to admire the view. Directly across from my building were the offices of the most prominent attorneys in Melbourne, and in one of them was the most beautiful woman I'd ever laid eyes on.

Even though we'd never spoken, I knew all about her. Her name was Audrey, and she was my secretary's flatmate—information I'd stumbled upon one evening as I was leaving the office. I saw the two of them running to catch the train, and I'd asked Amanda the following day who she was. She had even pointed out her office to me.

Every Friday in her office her lover would arrive, and every Friday I'd be at my window, watching, waiting to see her as only her lover did. They didn't disappoint me today, and as I reached for my binoculars I kicked my office door closed. Flicking the intercom switch, I spoke quickly to Amanda.

"No calls for the next hour, okay?" I snapped.

"Sure, Miss Jones," she replied.

It was a perfect summer's night, and I had a crystal-clear view of her office.

There they were, kissing and fondling each other. They had no regard for anyone else, and I often wondered if they knew they were being watched. I settled back in my chair to watch their lovemaking. The other woman took off Audrey's jacket and then unzipped her skirt, dropping them both to the floor. Audrey stepped out of the skirt, kicking it away from her feet. She wore a black bra and half-slip. Suspenders and stockings peeked out below the slip.

Audrey wiggled her way onto the desk, a stiletto heel visible as the other woman ran her hand up her leg and down the outside of her thigh, then back up under the slip. She threw her head back as though laughing, her dark hair spilling down her back. Her lover was at the hollow of her throat, then moved toward her breasts.

Audrey's hands held the woman's head while she pushed her biceps together, forcing her breasts to practically spill from their cups as her lover buried her face into them. The woman pulled back, and I watched mesmerized as she slowly stripped out of her clothing, down to her underwear. She knocked Audrey's legs open as she moved back toward the desk.

They embraced again, kissing and groping each other. My pussy throbbing, I shifted uncomfortably in my chair. The woman's hands were behind Audrey's back where they unclipped her bra, allowing her massive breasts to fall, swaying, as she discarded it.

She lifted each breast into the palms of her hands as though feeling the weight of them. Then she pounced on one, smothering it, kissing and licking, her tongue snaking around. She pulled back slowly. She had the tip of the nipple in her mouth and was stretching it out until Audrey's hands drew her head back in. Her mouth worked its way downward as her hands pushed Audrey backward until she lay flat on the desk. Audrey's breasts flopped down her sides, while the woman inched up the slip with her teeth to leave it bunched up at Audrey's waist.

The woman stood back then, looking down at Audrey as she picked something off the desk and ran it down her lover's abdomen. It must have been a letter opener, and with a quick flick of her hand she held up a flimsy G-string for her inspection.

I focused in harder and was rewarded as the woman sucked at the crotch of the G-string. Audrey's breasts jiggled as she laughed, the dark nipples rising and falling.

Audrey's breasts weren't the only things I wanted to zoom in on. She was such a magnificent-looking woman, her gorgeous dark hair framing the curves of her face. I desperately wanted to see her pussy, but as I continued downward, I could only see a dark tuft of pubic hair poking up between her suspenders.

I rubbed my pussy through my clothing, enjoying the sensation, fantasizing about her lying on my desk with her legs opened to me. A head came into view as the woman's long tongue snaked its way up and down Audrey's slit. Fuck, I was getting hornier by the second, and when Audrey lifted her legs and wrapped them around the woman's head to draw her closer into her, I pushed my hand into my panties, my fingers dipping into my hot, wet pussy.

I eased farther back in the chair, stretching my body out fully, opening my legs wide, slipping a few fingers inside, enjoying the warmth as I fingered myself. The erotic combination of spying and masturbating had me pushing my pelvis forward, imagining Audrey's fingers there and her mouth closing in on me.

Then a mouth was on me, ripping aside my panties, sucking,

licking, nibbling. I wrapped my legs around the head, forgetting for a moment where I was. Then reality hit, and I pushed the head away, straightening up in my chair.

"Please," my secretary, Amanda, begged. "I've been wanting..."

"You knew," I gasped.

"Of course. I've been waiting for the right time. Why do you think I pointed Audrey's office out to you?"

Her hands were on my breasts, her mouth seeking out mine. I lost control and grabbed her, pulling her onto the chair with me. It collapsed under our weight, and we fell to the floor laughing.

Ripping off our clothes we ravished each other, lying naked on the floor with perhaps all the occupants of the offices across the street looking on. I didn't care. I could only concentrate on our lovemaking. I knew that from now on there would be no need for me to watch someone else. It was time others were watching me.

MELT MY HEART

Lila Brooks

I spent all day struggling with the chocolate, melting and coaxing it, thinking of pouring it all over Gina's glistening body. Gina, my Gina, the maddening minx I'd fallen for three years ago. Our anniversary always falls right before Valentine's Day, and there's the temptation to let them just blend together, but I always insist that they're two separate and distinct events. Especially this year, because Gina's not even around. She had to go off on a business trip on the most romantic day of the year. I guess she could have gotten out of it—she could have quit. But she's not a quitter. She'd apologized profusely, said she'd be back the next day, and promised to bring me a gift from L.A. But I wanted her, not some Hollywood sign snow globe. Instead of moping, I did what I always do when I'm upset: I bake and cook.

I'd found my old heart-shaped molds and was melting down the chocolate, watching it go from a solid, sweet treat to a liquidy warm goo, dabbing my finger into the pot occasionally to taste the mixture before ladling it out. I was making tiny little hearts that were somehow supposed to represent mine, and the torrent of feelings I had for my girl, even more so now than at the start, even more so though I'd yelled at her as she walked out the door, hurt I'd have to be alone on this special day. Single people are alone on Valentine's Day, not couples. But after Gina had left, my words lingering in the air, echoing off the walls and back into my head, I wanted nothing more than to give her a final kiss, to tell her I was just upset because I would miss her. Instead I poured my heart out into the chocolates, and also into her favorite chocolate cake, measuring and mixing, pouring and stirring, until the entire apartment smelled like sugar and warmth and sweetness. I resisted taking too many bites, because the best part about my efforts in the kitchen is always sharing the results with her.

I checked the schedule to see what was on TV, figuring I'd go with some sappy Lifetime movie. I wanted to make sure the cake was perfect, the chocolates too; I imagined myself laying down a trail of red hearts from the front door to our room to greet her when she walked in. I was putting the finishing touches on the pink icing, swirling it until it appeared perfectly lush and creamy, when I heard a key in the door. I turned, startled, the long knife still in my hand. In walked Gina, all six feet of her tan, slim body, with a huge bouquet of roses. She wore a ravishing red dress that hugged every part of her. "Happy Valentine's Day!" she sang, running across the floor and flinging herself into my arms. She wrapped those athletic arms around my waist, almost knocking me into the stove.

"What are you doing here?" I asked her. "Aren't you supposed to be on a plane?"

"Nope."

Just "nope," no explanation, no additional information about why my beloved had suddenly rearranged my entire lonely night, one I'd almost started looking forward to. I laughed, overwhelmed with joy that I'd gotten what I wanted on this most precious of nights. But then I stopped myself, forcing a stern look onto my face, even though on the inside I was doing a little dance of glee.

"Nope?" I said. "That's all you have to say, after I've spent the whole day moping and baking and missing you? How long did you know you didn't have to work? I can't believe you didn't tell me."

My voice was getting louder and louder, and I found myself getting more and more worked up, and more and more turned on. "While you were zipping around," I told her, "I've been baking this cake and making chocolates for you. I think you need to get yourself in the bedroom right now and strip down to your underwear." I'd never spoken to Gina like this before, and while we'd dabbled in role-playing, sometimes really getting into it, we'd never mixed up our real life and our sex life before. But suddenly I was overcome with the most urgent desire to spank her sweet little ass. I wasn't mad at her really, but I felt the need to teach her some kind of lesson, and the truth is I love nothing more than giving her ass a nice, firm spanking.

Gina loves it too, which is why she dutifully scampered to the bedroom, and by the time I'd turned off the oven and set my chocolates to mold, she was facedown on the bed, naked save for a thin strip of ruffled red thong bisecting her perfectly curved ass. The sight of her nearly naked across our bed—so eager, so docile, so sexy—made my heart race and my pussy throb. I rubbed my hands in anticipation before joining her. I snapped her thong, taking a peek at her puckered hole before the fabric fell back into place. Then I squeezed her luscious asscheeks, which always brings out my desire to give them a few smacks.

For some reason I find that her butt looks better when it's a little bit red, and Gina certainly agrees.

I settled her across my lap, the better to feel her squirm, and doled out her much-deserved spanking. Actually, she didn't totally deserve it, but we both love to grapple with each other, and I genuinely had been crestfallen at the idea of spending Valentine's night alone, with only my cooking to keep me company. I summoned every bit of resentment I'd felt, as her heart-shaped ass turned a lovely shade of red.

"Gina," I moaned, overcome with the pleasure of feeling her round cheeks warm beneath my touch and her body squirming with pleasure. It was probably a toss-up as to which of us was wetter, though when I kept one hand firmly on her ass and plied her slippery folds with the other, she seemed to be winning that particular race. "Baby," I said, needing to enter her. I got up and fumbled for our favorite dildo, quickly getting it out of its hiding spot under the bed.

As soon as the toy slid inside her, I saw the change in my girl. Her body tensed, then relaxed, then tensed in a whole new way, accepting this welcome invasion and craving more. I was no longer punishing her for anything, but rather celebrating our love, our connection, and her gorgeous body, which never fails to turn me on, even when I'm angry with her. She always manages to make my anger melt away, until my insides are nothing more than a puddle, a liquid mess that only makes sense when she's near. Now, wielding the dildo with one hand, I spanked her with all the force I could muster, lifting my free arm and bringing it down with a passion I can only conjure for those who undo me in a vital, visceral way, for those I need so desperately I'll forgive them anything.

As I pressed the cock into Gina's pussy, watching her spasm around it, drawing it farther inside, I let my smacks roam, dipping down to her upper thighs, veering to the very edges of her asscheeks, taking her for as thorough a ride as possible. When she was right on the verge, I slid out the cock, hearing her whimper at the loss. I replaced it with my fingers and frantically thrust them into her. I moved so I could straddle her leg, pumping myself against it while holding her down. As I worked my fingers into her, I tweaked my own clit with my other hand. Feeling both of us so wet, so needy, and so desperate for each other was everything I could have asked for and more.

I silently urged her on, thrilled when I felt her pussy tighten around my fingers, clamping down so much they were squeezed together. I lay down next to her so I could look at her face while she came. Gina rolled over so we lay on our sides, face to face.

She kissed me while I sank my fingers over and over into her glorious wetness while continuing to probe my own. Touching myself is so much hotter when she's here to share it, and I cried out at how my night had almost turned out—alone, with me frosting a cake and molding chocolate into fake hearts while my real one ached for my true love. And here she was, coming in a series of spasms that left her gasping for breath, burrowing her head into my shoulder, pushing to get as close to me as she could. Her fingers snaked down to join mine, pushing inside my dripping wetness while I pinched and pulled and rubbed my clit. With our teamwork I came quickly, shuddering against her.

It was a long while before we got up and went back to the kitchen. Gina bounded forward, pouring my carefully made hearts out of their molds and back into the pot, then turning on the heat. "I worked hard on those. What are you doing?" I said, trying not to whine, and trying even harder not to pick a fight on this particular night.

"Baby, you've melted my heart so many times since I walked

through the door, it's only fair that I melt yours, too," Gina said.

I didn't tell her she already had. I just let her boil down the rich, sweet candy until it swirled around the pot, small bubbles forming on the surface. She let it cool just enough, then dipped her finger in and began to feed me the most delicious meal I've ever tasted. We feasted on melted chocolate, cake, and each other for the rest of the night, and long into the weekend.

LONELY TOWN

Radclyffe

There's nothing quite as lonely as a Saturday night in a strange town on the far side of midnight. In the last twenty-four hours, I'd crossed more than just time zones and thousands of miles—I'd shed one reality for another, let my ordinary life slip away like an unneeded cloak until I arrived halfway around the world a different person. No one knew me other than as the persona I allowed them to see. No one met me at the airport, because I wasn't scheduled to appear until the next morning. Until then, I was only a name on a program and a face on a flyer.

Too tired to sleep and too restless to read, I decided to go for a walk, ignoring the concerned expression on the night clerk's face as I crossed the lobby and stepped out into the dark. As was true in so many cities in the middle of the night, traffic was sparse and pedestrians rare. Nevertheless, the sidewalks were well lit by a combination of streetlamps, neon reflections from store signs, and a surprisingly bright gibbous moon.

I walked in the direction the cars were headed, the steady

thud of my booted feet on the empty pavement a welcome ac-
companiment, like the beating of another heart in a darkened
room. As soon as I turned the corner, I saw the bold, black letters of the stark white marquee a block away: GRAND HOTEL.
Why not? What better way to spend my last hours of anonymity
than with the woman who was famous for her secretiveness and
seclusion? As I approached the theater, I caught movement out
of the corner of my eye and turned to see a woman crossing the
street at an angle, her path on an intercept with mine. With the
lights behind her and her body shrouded in a long military-style
coat that came to just below her knees, I could see little of her
face and nothing of her body. I knew without doubt, though,
that she was a woman—I could tell by the singularly fluid grace
of her movements. She drew near with a purposeful stride, as if
she were late to meet me and eager to catch up. I slowed to wait,
as though our rendezvous were prearranged.

"Are you going to the theater?"

Her voice was husky, with a lilting accent that tinged her
English with a hint of Scandinavia. Closer now, I saw she was
indeed blonde, her eyes blue or green, too muted in the half-light
for me to be certain. Her coat billowed with each step, exposing
long legs in pale denim and a shirt unbuttoned far enough to
reveal that she wore nothing under it.

"Yes. Do think I'm too late?"

"No," she replied, extending her hand. "I think we're just in
time."

I took her hand as if I had a hundred times before.

Her fingers were long, slender, and cool. Her palm was soft
but with a faint ridge at the base of each finger suggesting that
she worked with her hands. I stole another glance at her face,
thinking that with her arched cheekbones and full jaw she might
have been a model. But there was nothing studied or posed

about her. She was at ease in her body in a way that those who made a living with theirs were not.

"Have you seen this before?" I asked.

Her full mouth curved into a secret smile. "Many times."

She moved even closer as we walked, until her shoulder and thigh touched mine, the way a lover's would, with familiarity and possession. I struggled not to close my fingers tightly around hers as a surge of desire caught me unawares and made me stumble.

"Are you all right?" she asked.

"Perfect," I replied, only then realizing it was true. At the first touch of her hand, I'd forgotten the disquieting sensation of being halfway around the world and a stranger to everyone, even myself. The parts of myself I'd left behind slowly reappeared, sliding into the empty places effortlessly until I remembered who I was and why I had come.

"Two, please," she announced as she passed several oddly colored notes through the semicircular hole in the Plexiglas to the bored-looking young man in the booth.

"Oh, no," I protested, belatedly realizing we had reached the theater while I had been lost somewhere between yesterday and tomorrow. "You must let me pay."

She laughed softly. "It is, as you would say, my treat."

I blushed furiously, not at all certain that she meant it the way I took it, but her words brought another flood of arousal from my depths. She cocked an eyebrow at me then swept her fingers lightly over my cheek and down my neck until her hand cupped my throat. She leaned close, there in the bright lights of the ticket booth, and skimmed her mouth over mine. "We should go in."

"Yes," I breathed, wanting nothing more than more of her mouth.

The lights went down just as we stepped into the theater, and she guided me through the blackness into the back row, to the far corner seats. There was no one in front of us or to the side. In fact, the other figures in the room were merely faint reminders that we were not alone. Distant images of Garbo and Barrymore flickered on the screen, their words a faint hum beneath the roaring in my ears.

Her coat fanned out behind her as she shrugged it from her shoulders, and when she extended her arm along the seat behind my back, the tips of her fingers grazed my shoulder. Each fleshy circle was a burning coal that penetrated the cotton to my skin. I leaned against her, and when my breast pressed to her side, my nipple tightened into a pebble of tingling nerves. She curled her arm and drew me closer, shifting to put her mouth against my ear.

"No one can see."

It wasn't true, but the illusion of invisibility beneath the otherworldly light in the cavernous space was enough. I tugged the shirt from her jeans and rested my hand on her belly. Her stomach tensed as I slowly rubbed my palm over the soft skin, pressing harder as the moments passed, my eyes on the screen but every sense tuned to her. The muscles beneath my fingers quivered and grew rigid, and with a faint moan, she shifted in her seat and spread her legs wide, her knee brushing mine. I knew she would be naked under the denim. The fingers that curved around my upper arm trembled. I could stop, but what would be the point? From the instant she'd taken my hand and I'd let her, our destination had been clear.

It was my turn to skim my lips over her ear, my breath a teasing kiss. "Are you hard already? Can you feel the seam brush against your clit, just like my lips caressing the tip?"

"Yes," I said, urgent and low.

My hand moved up, pushing fabric aside to cup her breast, grasping a nipple—already standing up, hard and sensitive, waiting. I squeezed gently. Once more. And again, harder, twisting a little until her body stiffened and another soft gasp escaped her. Her hips lifted, her heart skittering beneath my palm. I lowered my mouth to the other breast, biting through the soft cotton to tug on tender flesh. The gasp became a moan—hers or mine, I wasn't certain. My clit jerked insistently, keeping time with her racing pulse, and I finally dropped my free hand to my crotch and rubbed the stiff prominence through my pants.

"Open your jeans," I murmured against her neck as I drew my tongue along the curve of that beautiful jaw. Her breath, shallow and fast, drowned out the sound of Crawford's haughty inflections. I glanced down, saw her rip at the button and zipper, and squeezed the fabric between my thighs hard around my own aching need. My clit twitched, my vision blurred, and I had to ease off or come. I tortured her nipple a little more with my teeth to take my mind off the pressure in my clit.

Her eyes, suddenly bright and clear in the murky light, held mine.

"Please."

I stopped touching myself and pushed my fingers down the front of her pants as she rocked her hips, urging my fingers to find her. God, I wanted to take her fast—to make her come on my fingers, in my hand. I rested my fingertips just above the base of her clitoris, pressing down ever more firmly while circling up and down the stiff length, making it throb as the blood built inside. I knew how it felt, how it hurt in a way that could only be pleasure. Then, one hand stroking through that liquid heat below, I grasped her neck with my free hand and turned her face to mine. I worked my tongue into her mouth, the way I wanted to be working inside her. Turning in the seat, I threw one leg over hers. Clit pounding as I rode her leg, I sucked on her tongue the way I wanted her sucking on me. She bucked on my hand and moaned into my mouth and I forgot why I was waiting. Her need and mine conspired to undo me, and I surrendered willingly.

I pushed my hand deeper into her pants, my wrist tenting the denim until the zipper bit into my skin. Unmindful of the pain, I slid my fingers into her and angled my arm to get higher, crushing her clit, wet and hard, into my palm. Half laying on her now, my tongue in her mouth, my fingers buried inside, I took her hard and fast, beating her clit with the heel of my hand on each thrust. She pulled away from the kiss and closed her teeth on my neck when she started to come, muffling her cries with my flesh. She clamped down around my fingers as her hips jerked up, her rigid body barely touching the seat, and I felt a breathless, heart-stopping wonder as she came. I was ready to come, needed desperately to come, but in that moment, the only thing that I knew was her pleasure. Only when she slumped back into the seat with a last, long moan did the fury of my desire overtake me. I closed my hand around her still-pulsing sex and lowered my forehead to her chest. Dimly I was aware of her holding me as I shuddered and thrust against her tensed thigh. I choked on my own sobs of pleasure as a dam burst inside me and every barrier dissolved. I came in the arms of a stranger who knew me more intimately in that moment than anyone else in my life.

We dozed through the rest of the movie. I blamed my torpor on jet lag, but the truth was that I liked the way she held me. When the credits rolled, we straightened our clothing and left before the others. The streets were completely empty, and we walked in silence the few short blocks to my hotel. In the darkness beneath the awning, she leaned down and kissed me, the same knowing brush of lips with which she had first greeted me.

"Good night," she said softly.

I watched her walk away until the billowing edges of her coat became only the shifting shadows of the night. Then I turned and walked inside. It was not the Grand Hotel, and no grand passion awaited me here. But when I finally laid my head upon the crisp, white pillowcase, I felt her body next to mine, and her breath against my cheek. I closed my eyes, knowing I would not sleep alone.

WHAT SHE NEEDS

Jac Hills

The phone rings. It's a familiar voice: "I'm in town. Come to me and bring your toy bag."

I dress with care. It's important. I know what she likes, what she needs. Black silk boxers, black silk shirt, no bra, black leather trousers, and heavy black boots. I bring my toy bag as requested. I have some new toys—I know she'll like them.

This is not a date. There will be no predinner drinks, no meal. I arrive at the hotel and give her name at the front desk. I'm told to go right up, room 220. She opens the door. She's dressed in a crimson silk robe. It must be hers—this hotel is far too miserly to give its guests robes of any sort, let alone silk. It clings in all the right places. My mouth waters as she walks away from me toward a small table. The sheer fabric slides across her skin, outlining her breasts and buttocks. I can tell she's naked beneath it.

There are two bottles of beer in an ice bucket on the table.

Clever girl. She hands me one of the bottles. No words are spoken; none are required. We sit and drink the beers. When we've finished them off, she stands and slips the robe slowly from her shoulders and onto the floor. She kneels beside the head of the bed, and I know it has begun. She has given me total control.

I open my toy bag and spread its contents over the room's other bed. I haven't brought everything, just what I know she likes—plus my two recent acquisitions. The first: a new flogger, not leather like my other ones. This one is latex. The braids are thinner, its sting sharper—lighter and very erotic. I know: I've felt its blows caress my shoulders and back. That's where I love to feel it when I switch and play the sub. But there won't be any switching tonight. She needs a complete domme. Beside the whip I place a glass dildo, yet untried, but tonight we'll christen it. I take three candles—special ones, not the sort your local corner store sells. I light two and place them on either side of her bed, then turn off all the lights.

Should I order her to strip me? Or should I restrain her and give her a slow striptease? I pick up my leather restraints with the fur-lined wrist-cuffs and look at her. I can read in her eyes what she wants, but I haven't given her permission to speak, so she's biting her lip. I hesitate and consider giving her permission—maybe asking her what she wants—but I don't. She really is the total sub; if I ask her anything it'll spoil all of this for her. I don't want that. I want this to be good for her. So instead I fasten the cuffs around her wrists and point to the bed. She climbs onto it and looks at me to see whether I want her on her back or facedown. I press her shoulders slightly so she knows to lie on her back. Then I tie the restraints to the headboard and turn her head to the side so she'll have a clear view of me.

I stand back and strip for her, very slowly. First my boots, then my silk shirt. She bites her lip again as the soft candlelight glints off my nipple piercings. If she's good maybe I'll allow her to play with the rings later. I can see she wants the leather trousers to stay for a while, so I leave them, just opening the zipper a short way, enough to show the black silk beneath.

When I take out a blindfold, she whimpers. *Ah-ah, naughty girl.* She knows better than to make a sound without permission. I knew she wouldn't want to be blindfolded while I still had my trousers on. She'll have to be reprimanded for that. I tie the cloth over her eyes and fix restraints on her ankles, spread-eagling her completely. I can tell she's into the scene: she's glistening with arousal.

And I'm as wet as she is.

Now I can start in earnest.

I lean over her and blow gently across her chest. Her nipples, already firm, grow harder, more erect. She loves this—knowing something will happen but not what or when or where. I let her feel my leather trousers as I draw my right leg lightly over her thigh and pull myself around so that I can drag it over her abdomen. She can feel the leather but not the pressure. Then I pull back. Oh, she's very good—she doesn't make a sound.

I reach over and grab a mitten. This one is soft velvet. I prefer the velvet to fur, finding it more sensual on heated skin. I run my velvet-clad hand over her body, brushing her thighs, her hips, her breasts. I stroke across her engorged nipples very slowly, very softly. She's twitching already. She'll break soon. She must really need this.

Stepping back, I light the third candle and take some ice from the bucket that held the beer. I'm careful to make no noise, giving her no warning of what's to come. Starting at her shoulder, I allow the candle to drip onto her. As each drop of hot wax lands, I follow up with ice. Hot, then cold, as I work my way down her torso. No wax on her breasts, though, just ice. The first bite of cold on her nipple catches her by surprise and she gasps. More chastising will be required. When I reach her clit I rub what's left of the ice cube across it. Her body jerks, and I speak for the first time. "Did you come?" She shakes her head. "Good," I tell her, my voice a low growl. "You'd better not do that without my permission." She shakes her head again and shivers.

I remove the blindfold, and she watches as I finish stripping. I pull down the zipper with agonizing slowness, its sound loud in a room in which both of us are holding our breath. My body sings with tension. If I'm already this aroused she must be desperate to come. I'll let her, but not yet. She has some punishment coming first.

I release the restraints and roll her facedown, then fasten the cuffs again. I retrieve my new flogger. I know she likes it over her buttocks and hips. I trail its braids across her and then begin. Softly and gently at first I allow it to caress her, and she moves into its kiss. It's a good flogger—it has a beautiful sound. I can tell from the way she twitches that it feels good for her too. As my blows grow faster and harder I tell her, "You have my permission to make noise." She gasps. In relief? I don't know. And then she starts to moan, her sounds making me even wetter.

When her ass is nice and hot, I slow down again, ending as I started with a soft caress of the whip. I turn her face up again and decide to tease her really, really well before I let her come. It's what she likes best.

"Watch," I tell her. I lean back against the other bed and spread my legs. With one hand I open myself for her, giving her a clear view. She can see how wet she makes me. With the other I gently stroke myself along my slit. One finger dips just inside to gather moisture before returning the way it came, back up to my clit. I don't make a sound. I don't want to break her concentration—I just want to break *her*. My breathing hitches, though. I can't help it. With that one finger, I slowly circle my clit, putting the lightest of pressure on it. I'm not sure if she's still breathing, she's so still, but then she moans again. I desperately want to come. But I consider, what would tease her more? Stopping short. So I stop. Christ, it takes all my willpower. But this isn't about me. It's about what *she* needs. All the same, it takes a moment or two before I can stand and move to her again.

I've brought a linked pair of nipple clamps with me. The kind with teeth. I clip them to her nipples. Swollen as they are, it must hurt, but she groans in pleasure not pain. Or perhaps it's the pure pleasure that sometimes springs from pain. The chain between the clamps is long enough to put between her teeth. So I do, and I tell her not to move her head. I take the restraints from her ankles. She's so into what we're doing, I can control her without them. "Keep them spread," I tell her, tapping her legs to emphasize my meaning. And then I touch her. I run my fingers across her clit exactly the same way I did my own. She moves slightly, but she keeps her legs where I put them. I stop just before she can orgasm, and she whimpers again. I'll allow the sound; I did give her permission to make noise.

I get the glass dildo and show it to her. I can tell she's interested. It has to be held by hand and not strapped on. It's long and fairly thin and oh so smooth and cool. Just right against overheated flesh. I run the tip down, across her clit and as far as her opening. God, she's good. She's resisting pushing into it. I can see by the way her thigh muscles clench how much of an effort it is. But that isn't the game we're playing. She wants to break, she *needs* to break, to be unable to resist. And it's my job to take her there, to make her beg, to break her down until she's only need and heat and want.

I dip the tip of the dildo into her, just the tip, then move it around in a circle. She moans. I pull it out and she moans again.

She twitches, almost giving in—almost but not quite. I lay the dildo along her length and leave it there, letting go. The tip rests against the edge of her hole, the dildo itself stretched along her slit and sitting on her clit. Holding myself up by spread arms and toes, I suspend myself over her as much as possible without actually touching her. I nip, lick, and bite my way up her abs until I reach the beginning of the chain that links her nipples. I tug it gently with my mouth and she gasps. Then I rest one leg slightly on her—and on the dildo. Her hips move a little more.

It is enough.

"Please," she says.

"Please, what?" I lean and take my weight off her.

"Please, Master, fuck me. Please let me come. Please, I need to come. Please, Master." She breaks.

That's what I've been waiting for. That's what she needs to make this really good. I grab the dildo and slip it into her. It slides in smoothly—that's the beauty of glass. I fuck her with it, slow and smooth and deep. She's begging me the whole time. "Please fuck me. Please make me come." I do, and she does, shuddering and crying out. When she slumps down, spent, I slowly slide out the dildo and hold her.

She'll need more. She always does. And I need to come. I really, really need to come.

I take off her restraints. Neither of us needs them now. With my words alone I can control her. And she needs to let me. She needs to obey because she has no choice. With the illusion of compulsion gone she faces her own desires, acknowledging that this happens because she wants it. She is a bitch in heat because *she* needs it, not because I force her.

When she's ready I tell her to kneel on the bed with her head on the pillow and her ass in the air. I tell her to spread her legs and show herself to me, shameless yet vulnerable. Because she needs that too. She does as she's told. I fetch the harness—the heavy-duty studded leather one—and my Nexus double dildo. Sliding the smaller end into myself takes great control. I'm so close, so ready. God. But I do it, for her. I look at her as she displays herself to me. Her arousal glistens in the flickering light as her wetness seeps onto her thighs. "Touch yourself," I command, my voice thick with need. I watch as she strokes herself. She won't make herself come. She knows better than that. But before it gets too difficult for her I make her stop. I fuck her from behind, hard and fast and deep. By now, fending off my orgasm is pure torture, especially since I won't let her come until she begs again. She does beg, and I let her orgasm explode from her. She groans, shaking uncontrollably. As her orgasm overtakes her, I finally let mine claim me. If there's an earthquake report on the news tonight, think of us.

We rest for a while before I withdraw from her. She's ready to be eaten now. But before I start, I drip a little diluted peppermint oil into my mouth. I press the flat of my tongue against her cunt, and the heat of the oil takes her by surprise. Her breath catches, and she arches her back, almost coming. Her willpower impresses me as she fights to hold it back.

Then I lick her, letting my tongue slip along her folds as I taste her. I push the tip of my tongue inside her, just the tip, mindful of the peppermint oil and that she's probably sensitive from the fucking. I sweep my tongue over her, the flat of it dragging along her lips then the tip flicking swiftly from side to side. I circle her clit, tease it, taste it. I let my teeth graze it, but I don't bite—she's too sensitive for that—and she gasps. I could do this for hours, but I feel her build toward release again. I keep flicking her clit with the edge of my tongue. She's ready. I suck in her clit, draw it between my lips. Her body rises from the bed, balanced on her heels and the crown of her head, as massive shudders ripple through her and a single word is forced through clenched teeth: "Christ."

I let her rest as I clean the toys and put them away. When she's back in her body—and in this world where walking and talking are possible again—we shower. I wash her and pat her dry with the hotel's fluffy towels. I gently massage lotion into her skin, noticing again how soft she is.

We curl up together on the bed as the first signs of dawn lighten the room. In a little more than two hours I'll leave for work. I'll kiss her good-bye and she'll blush shyly, as if we're strangers to raw sexuality and have never spent time wrapped together in this sensual haze. And she'll smile and say, "See you in six months or so?"

I'll grin and reply, "Sure."

But for now I'll cradle her in my arms and let her sleep. Because that's what she needs.

GEEK CHIC

Gina Klein

Never in a million years did I think I'd pick up the girl of my dreams at the Apple store, that geek Mecca in Soho. But that's exactly what happened. I have to admit, I'm the furthest thing from a computer nerd you can find. I know how to check email, use iTunes, and visit the latest gossip websites, but when it comes to anything more heavy-duty than plugging in my laptop, I'm clueless. I only use the Apple store to check my email and use the bathroom, hustling past lines of avid shoppers and technologically savvy customers.

Upstairs there's a tiny theater where the store sometimes holds classes or panels. I'd walked past it dozens of times on my way to the restroom, with nary a glance at the instructor. This time, though, a voice caught my ear, and I looked to find an exquisite-looking woman leading a class of interested students through the ins and outs of building a website. I couldn't take my eyes off her. She wasn't drop-dead gorgeous in the usual sense, but something about her completely drew me in, something tough and alluring. She was olive-skinned, probably Hispanic, and her black hair was cropped short, almost boyish but with a feminine twist, a studied diagonal swath across her forehead. The ends of her hair brushed across her neck, teasing me with the skin they left uncovered. She wore a black leather cuff around her wrist, a simple black tank top, and jeans. I couldn't tell her age; maybe she was in college or, like me, in her early thirties. All I knew was that my heart beat a little faster, and suddenly I was intent on learning everything I could about HTML. I raced to the bathroom, then returned and took a seat on the side so I could stare at her without her noticing too much.

I watched her work the room, and as words like *operating system*, *browser*, *hyperlink*, and *search engine* left her lips, I pictured those lips being put to a much better use. I shifted in my seat, afraid everyone could tell my interests were far more than technological. The woman, whose name tag said SONIA, led the class through creating a simple site, took questions, and seemed made for the stage. She didn't talk too fast or too slow, and she altered her lesson based on what people seemed to want to know. I was half-listening—since she made the material actually interesting—and half-watching the way her jeans clung to her ass perfectly, not too tight, not too loose.

Her breasts were on the small side, but that just made me hunger more to touch them, and I was lost in thought, imagining her naked, her rosy nipples begging to be tasted. I must have gotten more lost in my daydream than I'd imagined because all of a sudden I heard applause. The class was over. I gathered myself together, trying to think of an intelligent question that wouldn't make me sound like a total idiot.

I waited for everyone else to finish asking questions, then finally approached Sonia, figuring inspiration would strike me at the moment. I fingered the pendant on my necklace, a simple amethyst stone, for good luck. "Hi," I said, trying to hide my nervousness. "That was really great. I've never thought much about having my own site, but it sounded so easy during your presentation. I think I might try it."

"Great," Sonia replied enthusiastically. "I really think it's one of those things anyone can do." Her voice was husky but not too deep, sexy without even trying. She reached out and lightly touched my arm. "And if you need any help, I'm always here."

"Thanks," I told her, wracking my brain for what to say next, not wanting our conversation to end. "I'm Gina," I said, still thinking. "I live nearby, so I'm sure you'll see me again."

"I hope so," she said, her voice even deeper as she said those three promising words.

"Listen, I hope this doesn't sound weird," I told her, "but if you want to get a cup of coffee sometime..." I trailed off, uncertain as ever how to approach girls who made my mouth dry and my pussy wet at the same time.

"Is it really coffee you're after, Gina?" This time her innuendo was unmistakable. Sure, I'd approached her, but when it came down to it, I couldn't muster the courage to seal the deal.

"No, it's not," I said quietly. Then I just stood there, unable to get the second part of my thought out of my mouth, sure she had to know from my eyes as they darted from her to the floor to the other side of the room.

"Do you want to come home with me, Gina? Is that why you're acting like this?" Her voice was calm as she stared me down. She was so hot I was tempted to run away, unsure I could handle being alone with such a strong, proud, sexy woman. Most of the girls I'd been with were similarly shy and awkward, and we'd laugh about that as we made out. But kissing Sonia was no laughing matter.

It was do-or-die time. I stepped closer so that I could feel her breath on my face. Without touching her, I looked her straight on and said, "Yes, I want to come home with you."

"Meet me out front in five minutes," she said, her tone changing, becoming more businesslike, the way it had sounded in front of the crowd earlier. I liked this take-charge Sonia, who seemed to have all the answers.

I went outside, trying not to get hit by the hordes of shoppers rushing past me. I got a soda from the hot dog cart just to have something to do, sipping the soft drink and letting its fizzy bubbles soothe me.

Wearing a light black jacket, Sonia finally emerged, and I followed her. We walked in silence while I checked her out. I wondered what she'd be like in bed, if that's where we were going. Maybe she was just inviting me over to get to know me better? I shook my head, as if to erase the thought. This was New York, and women here, dykes especially, move faster than that.

She led me several blocks away to a tiny studio apartment, nevertheless covetable by Gotham standards for its precious location. The only place to sit was on the bed, so I did.

"Tell me, what was it about me that attracted you today?" she said, putting me on the spot immediately. She sat right next to me, her fingers running along the seams of my jeans, playing with a stray thread. I wondered if she was nervous too.

"I liked how you took charge of the class," I told her. "But you weren't bossy or anything like that. You just knew what you were doing." She stared at me, perhaps her way of testing me. I gazed silently back at her, perhaps my way of letting her know she could control me, like she had her class.

"And you like that, Gina? You like it when someone else is in charge?" she asked, this time moving closer so her hand brushed my arm. Her body leaned toward me, ready to pounce.

"Yes," I told her, unable to say anything else as her fingers slid down my arm, stroking my wrist with her thumb as she captured it in her grasp. Again and again she stroked that one tender spot in the center of my wrist, near my palm, until I couldn't stand it anymore and tried to pull away—not because I didn't like it, but because her touch had such a hypnotizing effect on me.

"Where do you think you're going?" She held me tighter then reached for my other wrist. I offered them both to her, bringing my arms together, giving her a silent signal that I was hers. "That's more like it," she said. "You want me to take over, I will, but you should remember that old saying: be careful what you wish for."

With my arms caught in hers, Sonia pushed me onto my back. I was fully dressed but felt bare as her eyes took in all of me, not missing a trick as they wandered from my tight red sweater, the edges of my black bra peeking out, to my even tighter jeans, which I probably wouldn't have worn had I known I'd be lying on the bed of one of the hottest women I'd ever seen. She took one hand away from the wrist it was holding, letting me know with her eyes that she wanted me to leave it above my head.

Sonia's hand traveled down my arm, slowly filling me with her heat as she made her way to my waist, where she burrowed beneath my sweater to touch the spongy flesh above my hip. She lingered there, massaging the far reaches of my stomach with her thumb while I breathed heavily, looking up at her as she surveyed me. I wanted desperately to meet her approval, to make this adventure worthwhile for both of us lest I give in to my potentially ridiculous urge to back out, hop up, and run away. She waited me out, though, and stroked me gently. Her other hand roamed up my sweater, lightly stroking my breast until I gave in, my body relaxing fully into her touch, my spine unwinding as I offered myself to her.

Somehow Sonia could tell, and as I let out the breath I hadn't realized I'd been holding, her hands clamped over my rib cage, then pushed my sweater up to my neck. I made a move to take it off entirely, but she stilled me. "Keep your hands over your head, Gina," she told me, and the way she said my name, like some kind of curse, made me shiver. She peeled down the lacy layers of my bra, exposing my breasts and very quickly much more. "*Dios mio, chica*," she said, lapsing into Spanish at the sight of me, even though English was clearly her preferred language. It sounded so sexy to my ears, but soon I stopped listening almost altogether as my moans drowned her out.

She squeezed my breasts, making me wet my panties and arch my hips, and tugged on my nipples, pinching them tighter and tighter as my face contorted involuntarily. I swallowed hard and shut my eyes. She pressed hard against my nubs, while my jeans pressed tightly against my cunt as I twisted around. Sonia leaned down and grabbed one nipple between her teeth, sinking them into my pink flesh slowly but forcefully while her fingers did the same to my other nipple. Again she waited me out, pouncing on me as she pushed me to the limits of my arousal. I let out a strangled cry as her teeth crowded my nub, the pain sinking in above the pleasure, and just then she let go, her tongue assuaging the pressure she'd just created. If Sonia was on a quest to make me come by playing with my nipples, she was doing a good job.

I'd given up on trying to reciprocate in any way, because her powerful focus had turned me to jelly. She ran her lips all along my breasts then moved lower, licking along the ticklish rounded edges of my stomach, squirreling her tongue under my waistband. Finally she pressed the back of her hand against the wet seam of my jeans, rubbing my slit as I'd wanted her to do from the start. She pressed hard, the bony edges of her hand firm against my slick, needy lips. I think I cried out, "Yes" and later "Sonia," but I knew she would go at her own pace.

After torturing me with these clothed strokes for a while as I teetered on the edge of the waterfall, threatening to spill over but staying on the safe side for the moment, she peeled off my jeans and took my soaked panties with them. I was so wet that all I cared about was her touch, and Sonia didn't disappoint. She pushed one finger into my dripping wetness, and I heard her let out a moan, then a real curse as she inserted another and another. My arms still above my head, I banged my fists lightly against the bed, spreading my legs as her fingers sank magically inside. Out of the corner of my eye I saw some lube nearby, reached for it, and delicately tossed it over to her. I was plenty wet, but I wanted more. She slid her fingers out, and I felt the loss immediately, but when I opened my eyes and saw her drizzling lube onto her fingers, I was more than placated.

Sonia returned to my pussy, a look of studious arousal on her face as she again entered me, this time with three slippery fingers. I contracted around her, tightening against this much-needed pressure. She slipped her little finger inside, and I felt it edge its way along my walls. No sooner had I adjusted to that last digit than her thumb was nudging against me, pressing inside. Tears of pleasure pooled in my eyes when I realized she was going all the way: her whole hand. I shut my eyes and tried to stay as still as possible.

Sonia pressed her face against me, her tongue lightly stroking my clit as her fingers easily curled inside me until the tight ball of her hand was simply there, a fullness like nothing I'd experienced. If I opened my eyes, I could see her sinewy, muscular arm rocking minutely as she gently moved her powerful fist and her tongue kept pace with my clit. But what made stars explode behind my eyes, what made Sonia seem like a superhero, was when her free hand came around to press against my stomach. At first my hand reached up to stop her. The swelling and pressure were too great, too much, and I was afraid of what I might do. Would I crush her? Hurt her? Scare her? The Sonia in front of me wasn't just the sexy computer geek I'd glimpsed earlier, but a woman who was huffing and sweating, taking me over and over the most dangerous of precipices, giving so much of herself I could barely stand to accept it.

I didn't wonder why she was pulling out all the stops on what could only charitably be called our first date but simply went with the feeling, opening my body to her as she gently twisted her hand back and forth, knocking on my door, begging for entrance, even as her powerful palm pushed down against me. She was pushing and pulling, inside and out, everywhere at once, and when I finally did fall over that cliff and ride the sparkling white crashing waves to the ground, I screamed, my cries echoing off her walls as she flattened her tongue against my clit and guided me safely to the ground. My pussy clamped tightly around her hand, as if molding itself to her shape, while my juices trickled down her wrist. Who knows how long it went on—all I can tell you is that I was spent when we were done. I couldn't talk, and even if I'd wanted to, I had no idea what to say.

Sweetly, Sonia kissed me—on my hip, then my chest, then my shoulder, then my cheek—before getting up. She returned sparkling clean bearing a glass of water, and she helped me sit up and held the cool glass to my lips. "I don't know what to say," I finally managed, knowing she'd understand.

"I'm the one who's used to being in front of the mike, remember?" she said, her deep brown eyes teasing me as I struggled to sip instead of gulp.

That was two years ago, time during which I've seen Sonia work many crowds, flirting and teaching and showing off that gorgeous body as effortlessly as she slipped her hand inside me that first night. The only thing that's changed is that I've managed to show her a trick or two as well, but she's still my favorite geeky girl, and I'm happy to say I'm hers as well.

A NEW
NECKLACE

Austin J. Austin

Dalia was long past the tuning stage when I walked through the door. I recognized one of her new songs coming out of the amp, and I smiled. "Sorry I'm late. Sounds good."

She smiled at me and kept playing. I dug the thickest sheaf of poems out of my bag and looked for a clean place to sit. Jay and Kadja were lying propped up against each other on the futon. When I had closed the door, Jay had opened her eyes and taken a film canister out of the pocket of her hoodie. Now she picked up Kadja's limp hand, tapped some powder out onto the web between thumb and forefinger, sniffed a bump, and nodded up at me. When Kadja woke up and Jay told her, "I didn't want you to feel left out," the couple dissolved into sleepy kisses and giggles.

I settled onto one of Smith's famous dark-wood desk chairs with the wide seat, heavy frame, and inexplicable lower-leg tilt. Snide upperclasswomen-with-a-Y called it the Plath Tilt while looking up, for effect, at the ceiling for a pipe sturdy enough to toss a noose over. I had developed quite a penchant for sitting naked in mine, tipped all the way back, while getting eaten out. I'd hold on to my partner's long hair for balance, as ze sucked my clit and bit my luscious fat labia, and when I came I'd slide almost all the way off on my own juices.

Thinking of a mouth over my crotch made my cunt grow warm and my nipples harden. I breathed deeply and looked over at Dalia, hunched over her black Fender Telecaster with the punk rock stickers and white pick guard, her feet moving rhythmically in their untied striped sneakers. I'd missed her over the summer. Sometime in June she sent me a postcard from her favorite diner in her Los Angeles neighborhood, talking about the gig she'd had the night before. I carried that postcard in my bag with me for weeks until it nearly fell apart and my partner laughed at what a crush I had. "That's not true," I'd said, even if I could taste her skin in my every dream. "But even if it were true, we're only friends."

Dalia and I were friends, even though most of her friends, lovers, and girlfriends were much tougher than I, who had little interest in drugs and guns. We were college friends who valued each other's voices, art, ideas, and kindness, but I doubted we would value, say, each other's scent in the middle of the night. And though my primary partner was certainly not a man, I'd never slept with what I considered a woman before, a woman in the traditional sense, the double-X-labeled-at-birth sense, the bleeding-uterus-like-a-sacred-heart sense. Where Dalia'd had a hundred women since she started fucking at fourteen, I hadn't put more than kisses on one since I'd come out a year earlier. I didn't want to tell her, and I didn't want her to think she'd have to teach me anything.

Dalia turned on the four-track and we started putting lyrics and music together. Her band had just signed a two-record deal, but she still liked playing casually with me. We'd gotten together at least weekly during our first year, listening to the end results at the end of every session, our heads pressed together as we shared one set of studio headphones. I loved the resonance of Dalia's enormous voice and could hardly ever believe that she wasn't a foot taller—rather than a foot shorter—than I was. This night was no different. The lovers on the futon hardly stirred as we experimented and harmonized and laughed.

As always, Dalia and I ran out of tape, which signaled the end of the session. We soon got into a loud, heated conversation about the likelihood of Andrea Dworkin becoming a porn star before we realized it was past midnight and Dalia's roommates probably had their own midterms to take in the morning.

"Come to my room for a beer," I said. Unlike Dalia, I had a room of my own, of which Virginia Woolf would have approved.

"Sure, sounds good."

I pulled a hardpack of menthols out of my bag while I was putting my writing away. I tapped it hard against the palm of my hand and watched Dalia unplug her guitar and place it on its stand. By the time she was done, a red mark had formed just above my wrist, and Dalia came over to look. She touched the mark with one finger. Her eyes met mine, and she smiled slowly up at me. I swallowed hard and gestured with my head toward the door. The fluorescent hallway lights whined at us as we turned the corner.

My key turned over the tumblers very slowly as I unlocked the heavy wooden door to my room. At this time of night, the slightest noise was amplified in echoes that hit every door of every sleeping student on the hall. Somehow, tonight, it felt like a dozen eyes were watching me, but it could have been just

Dalia's two, looking at me calmly, which made me move self-consciously into the dark room.

I pulled the chain on the light and was able to see the detail on her white wifebeater. As usual, her tits bounced against her slim rib cage as she talked and laughed, her pierced nipples temporarily restrained by the fabric covering them. I handed Dalia a beer from the small fridge and turned on the stereo. I offered her a cigarette before lighting one for myself. I had the rough brown end in my mouth and flicked the lighter's silver wheel before I noticed she was looking intently at me. I inhaled deeply, my cheeks going slightly concave around the filter. As I sat next to her, I noticed she had three bruises on her left arm.

"Did you get those from rugby?" I asked her.

Dalia smiled at me, a little too sloe-eyed and deeply, as she smoked. "Something like that." She turned her left arm out further and brought it closer to me. At this angle, I saw two additional bruises, muted blue patches against her light skin, and I couldn't stop myself from wondering which lover had grabbed her so roughly. Before I could ponder this thought too long, Dalia brought that arm over my shoulder, resting her hand on my shirt, touching me all the way from my collar to the edge of my cuff. Her hand rested on the tender skin of my inner elbow where my pulse was jumping. I stretched my fingers to touch her in return, and her fingers bent in on themselves slightly, her nails making contact with my flesh as she pulled them down my forearm, hard. I gasped and arched my back before she scratched me again, this time with both hands, the cigarette hanging loosely from her lips. My eyes, wide at first, shut tightly as I processed the sensations accompanying the red lines on my skin.

Even then I didn't realize we were fucking. It took me until she knelt up over me, grabbed my cigarette and my beer, and then crushed her lips down over mine to figure it out. Until then

I thought she was roughhousing with me like I'd done with a thousand others, but after that point, after her tongue parted my lips and her teeth pulled my lips between them, I knew. My hands found her hips, and she pushed my hair behind my ears.

Then she slapped my face. My mouth fell open, and my head swung to the right. She didn't touch me again right away, instead letting the blood rise up in her handprint and my chest give a shudder. I knew by the look on her face that she was waiting for some sign of assent, so I nodded at her. Dalia licked her lips with no small amount of desire, and I pushed her shirt up to her neck. I thought she would slap me again for sure, so I was almost disappointed when she pulled my mouth to first one hard nipple and then the other. My lips pressed into her soft small breasts as I worked over her nipples with my teeth and tongue. We moved in time with the music, something like a lap dance, something like a floor show, something right out of a music video. Except she was so hot, her mouth felt so good on my neck, and she was real, covering my body with both scratches and caresses.

I could smell her, and my mouth and cunt watered equally. I undid the buckle on Dalia's studded belt, and the leather whistled as she slid it out of her pant loops. As I unzipped her pants, she slipped the belt around my neck, and as I removed the last of her clothes, she cinched the belt down hard, pulling me close to her, guiding my face to her neck, her breasts, her belly, and finally her pussy, which was framed with gold curls and steel. I tried to take a deep breath, but she was tugging on the belt, and my mouth quickly collided into those warm wet lips. I played my tongue across the slit between her pussy lips and brought her juice up to my lips, licking myself. As I pushed myself between Dalia's lips, she moaned and said, "My clit's kinda big." She wasn't kidding—almost an inch around it seemed as I rolled it around my lips like a jawbreaker. Her hand gripped the belt around my neck with a strength that left me scared, panting, and dripping wet. I felt her thighs shaking underneath my hands and licked more slowly and forcefully. She seemed to be getting close, but my vision was getting sparkly around the edges and I wanted to make her come before I missed out on it entirely.

I made a tight seal around her clit with my lips, watching to see if she'd respond. She bucked her hips into my face, and I stuck my tongue out for her to rub herself against. Almost instantly she let out a long soprano moan and started to come. At first she tightened her grip on the belt even harder, but she finally let go. I sank to the bed facedown, panting into her pussy, endorphins and oxygen rushing through my body.

I had no strength to fight her as she flipped me on my back. I didn't want anything but her mouth on me—anywhere. She tore off my pants and shirt, let her eyes and hands wander over my sizeable chest and tattoos, and said, "What do you like?" I asked her to kiss me, and as she did she put a thigh against my wet cunt. Between kisses, thrusts, and tugs on the belt around my neck, I managed to tell her I wanted her to lick my clit and hurt me a little. She smiled at me, almost enough to make me regret it, then put her head into my cleavage, sucking at my skin hard enough to leave long trails of bruises.

Dalia's hands traveled up my thighs, across my belly. She placed her fingers on the outside of my cunt, then brought them to my mouth for me to suck. I writhed against her, and she made no move to touch me further. The ache in my cunt forced me to whisper, "Please."

"Please what?"

I had no idea what to ask for. My cheeks burned, and I could hardly look her in the eye. I was hard and butch and not accustomed to asking, certainly not so desperately, and it made me feel very helpless and hot. "Please, will you fuck me?"

All at once, she was right in my face, licking my mouth. I tried to draw measured, deep breaths, but it was no use. I stopped fighting and tried to focus on what she was doing. Dalia grabbed a candle from the windowsill and lit it. Straddling my hips, she lit another cigarette from the flame and sat over me, smoking, watching me. She blew minty smoke over my engorged nipples, and I sighed with pleasure. She let me have a drag, and I savored the smoke before blowing it toward the ceiling. Then she grabbed her beer bottle and touched it experimentally to my left side. The cold made me buck and cry out, but I was pinned under her strong body. She grinned and dragged the cold, wet bottle across my chest, and by the time she poured drops of wax from the candle onto my chest, I was sobbing loud enough for the whole floor to hear. She put out her cigarette then downed the last sips of beer with her hand over my mouth.

Dalia got off me, moving her head down between my thighs. The beer bottle rolled down my chest and belly, settling to rest against my damp mound, round and open like DJ headphones. I felt her press the cold glass gently against my lips, which was a soothing, exhilarating sensation. I started to move my hips, and Dalia slapped my thigh. Immediately, I froze. Dalia's mouth was up against my cunt now, licking all the way inside me. It was the most wonderful thing, having her tongue curled and moving into my wet hole. She replaced her tongue with fingers, and I gasped uncontrollably.

"What is it?"

"That—that feels amazing!"

I felt her smile into my clit. "Oh, that? That's pretty, well, tame." My heart sank, and I blushed furiously. I felt so naïve and exposed, wanting to roll over and hide, but Dalia wouldn't let me go. I felt another finger sink into me and her tongue slide over my clit, licking it softly, bottom to top, just how I like it.

She growled into me, biting and pulling on my labial piercing. I was afraid of all she could do to me that I hadn't even imagined yet, and that fear opened my hole even wider with desire.

My mouth opened with a ragged breath that amped itself into near hyperventilation. P. J. Harvey sang on and on in the background, and when Dalia put the biggest part of her hand inside my tight gash, my howls matched that agonizing part in "The Dancer" where it sounds like P. J.'s getting fisted by the devil.

Dalia reached into her pants pocket and took out several metal picks. She put them over her fingers, and her face went back to my cunt. That left hand returned to its previous steady tempo inside my wet hole, while the other scraped and scratched and stabbed at my tits, belly, thighs, and arms with its metal adornments. I looked down to see her licking and fucking me, but what made my heart race faster was the sight of her raising dark welts on me. The liquid ascent that preceded my orgasms was beginning; I felt it rise higher in my belly, but with all that there was jammed inside my hole, there was nowhere for that orgasm to go but out my mouth with a force large enough to summon campus police if I hadn't thought ahead and jammed the pillow between my lips as I came. Dalia held gently but firmly onto the end of her belt until I stopped thrashing.

All too soon, Dalia slowly loosened the belt from my neck. I touched my neck where the belt had been, and it felt raised and hot like a halo.

Dalia yawned and ran her hands hard over her shaved head. She put her pants back on, rethreading her belt in the worn loops, and as she went looking for her shirt, she realized it had been underneath me as she fucked me, and that it was now wet with me. She smiled and picked up the shirt I'd been wearing, a black Sticky Fingers tee from my first time living in Baltimore, and asked if she could borrow it. I nodded, unaware I'd never see that shirt again and that she'd left the sort of girl-fucking artifacts in my room I'd later come to expect would be left behind: boxer briefs, a thick steel-bead chain, and a signed first edition of *The Complete Hothead Paisan*.

I stood to kiss her good-bye, and she once again became the sweet and bouncy rebel nerd I was accustomed to adoring. She pressed the power button on the stereo and silently let herself out. I found her necklace on the floor and put it on so it rubbed against my aching, bruised neck. Beyond the fucking itself, this talisman symbolized that I had been initiated, but into what I was still unsure.

The phone rang the double ring of an off-campus call. I rolled over and picked up. At this hour it would either be the Whispering Woman or my partner. The odds were slightly in my favor.

"Oh, my God. You'll never guess who I just had sex with."

"Never, eh?" A low chuckle, and then my partner read me an excerpt of the email ze had sent Dalia, a description of my crush on her and a suggestion that I would be up for a romp if invited.

Not even when I found my name in the liner notes for Dalia's first album a few months later did I feel so very loved. "Thank you very much," it said, using my girlie given name, which of course brought me no end of shame and joy.

THE FLAME

Tonne Forquer

The autumn trees and earth fill my vision as I stroll across the park. My eyes are heavy and my head swims with last night's desire. I spot a woman in the distance and I pray it's Amanda. Just the thought of her makes me wet. With each step I'm a little closer. I have a terrible need for my fix and no one else can quench it. My heartbeat quickens. It's her.

Amanda's standing outside her van, one hand on her hip, the other holding a cigarette. Her blue eyes and full lips against her pale young flesh and dark red hair drive me wild. I flash her a smile and bite my bottom lip.

"I was wondering if you were going to show." She grins and flicks the cigarette to the ground. Smoke escapes her mouth and floats into the early morning sky.

I hug her, and she rubs the back of my neck. As I take in her scent, my mind wanders. I want to melt in her arms, to ignore the rest of the world. I plant a gentle kiss on the back of her neck, and she lets out a soft moan.

She pulls me into the van. The windows are tinted black. We can see out, but the revelers in the park can't see she's doing a line from the tabletop or that I'm changing into a black dress. A Hole mix CD is playing on the stereo. She lights a red candle and kisses me on the forehead. Her grin widens.

Amanda likes me to dress up like a Goth girl. She pats her lap and I sit atop her with my black dress and blood-red lipstick. My skin is powdered pale, and my eyes look bruised. I love for her to take control of me, love to feel her commanding hands. Her energy once made me nervous, but now it excites me. I learned to love it as she loves me.

With my back to her, she puts her hand inside my panties to make sure I'm ready. She pulls my head to one side. I hear the click of a switchblade, and I let out a gasp as the cold steel touches my throat. She slides the knife beneath the sides of my panties and cuts them off. My back arches, and she spreads my legs. My breath is coming so fast. My eyes follow the knife, and she points it to my throat.

"You've been a bad girl," she growls. "I know you've been out with her again. I'm going to fuck you until you're raw so that bitch can't have you!"

I try to get up from Amanda's lap, but she grabs me and pulls me tightly to her, presses the knife against my neck again. I squirm in her lap. I want her so bad.

She slowly bends me over the edge of the table and teases my entrance with the head of her strap-on. She pushes into me with every breath.

"I'm sorry, baby," she whispers.

Our moans wash over each other with each movement. Amanda slides me back onto her lap. "Open your eyes," she says. "Watch the flame. Mimic its movement." I feel her sweat mingle with my own. She pricks her finger with the knife, drags her finger across a line of cocaine, and sticks it in my mouth. She drops the knife and digs her fingers into the flesh of my leg. She drives herself deeper into me as I bounce on her lap.

"Don't take your eyes off it." Her breathing grows heavier.

I drink her in. I want all of her. I watch the flame as it dances and sways just as we do. She runs her hand through my dark hair and slowly pulls my head back, bites my neck.

"What do you see?" she says forcefully.

"Mmmm...I...I..." is all that escapes me. I'm numb with pleasure. I can barely keep my eyes focused as she licks the back of my neck.

She puts her hands on my waist, tugging me down, allowing me to completely engulf this extension of her womanhood.

"You see us," she whispers. "And that is all you'll ever see again when you look at fire."

I turn around and kiss her. Our tongues entwine, and I straddle her once more. She enters me again and rocks back and forth until I climax. I'm in a daze as I enjoy her mouth and continue to ride her. I come twice more.

She looks at me with satisfied eyes, breathes in and nods her head. "Only you and me. Do you understand?"

She nudges me to the floor and wiggles the strap-on in my face. I take the head of it into my mouth, suck on the tip, and look up at her, seeking acceptance. She wants control of me again. She pushes my head down and fucks my throat until tears flow from my eyes. I feel her coming, and I push away. She knows I hate this, but it only makes her want to do it more. She kisses my cheeks and slowly licks the tears from them. She smiles at me and I focus on the lipstick prints I've left on her neck. My mouth finds hers again. I want to be lost.

Amanda removes the shaft from her harness, and she rubs my head. I eagerly lap at her pussy, my tongue desperately seeking her out. I pull my head back, her hand cradling the back of it and gently tugging my hair. I steal a glance at the dragon tattooed on her arm and look up at her. I want her to make me eat her pussy because it turns me on. And she knows this.

"I love you, baby girl." She smiles and pushes me into her. I stick my tongue in as far as I can, teasing her insides and pulling back out.

Amanda's so wet that a tenacious stream forms a bridge from her cunt to my mouth. I tease her clit until she comes. In the end, I know I'm the one in control.

"I am fire." She grins, almost laughing maniacally as she throws her head back.

She blows the candle out, gives me a rose, and kisses my forehead.

ROUTE 66

Lori Simmons

Kerry has a thing for waitresses. I think it's because they bring her coffee, which I never do—and then she gets to stare at their asses as they trot away. "We're staying in the motel next door tonight, but we're probably taking off in the morning," she says to a cute, blue-eyed, freckly girl.

This particular waitress isn't my type at all. She's very slim and girly. She seems like a cool person, but she isn't registering on my sexual radar.

But she's obviously registering on Kerry's.

"You're so sweet," Kerry says in response to an offer of sugar for her coffee. "Why don't you just stick your finger in there and twirl it around?"

"Oh, Christ. I can't believe you just said that," I murmur.

But the waitress smiles. I try to distance myself from the cheesy pickup line by lighting a cigarette. I love that Bob's Big Boy has a smoking section. I look into the mirror next to our booth. My roots need a touch-up, my hair is getting long, and the blonde highlights are a bit faded—but I'm wearing my favorite dress. It's stretchy black wool, knee-length, long-sleeve, and zips up the back. It only has a few holes in it. I'm probably too covered up for Kingman, Arizona, even in January. But this dress was the only clean thing I had. Kerry and I have been on the road for three weeks and haven't stayed in one place long enough to do a load of laundry. Kerry is wearing a threadbare Harley T-shirt and dangerously low Levi's.

The waitress is, of course, wearing her uniform. She fills Kerry's cup to overflowing and says, "I get off at six," before walking away with an exaggerated swish.

I give Kerry a pointed look and say, "I need something a little more substantial than pussy for dinner." But she knows I'm playing with her.

She pats my hand and says, "Drink your coffee, baby. We've got a few hours to kill. Why don't we go back to the motel?"

We picked this Best Western out of the *Damron Women's Traveller,* so I'm not really surprised to see another dyke couple in the hot tub. They're pretty attractive. In fact, the butcher of the two is pretty damn hot.

I can tell Kerry is getting antsy for some fun. That's my girl. She's got a nonstop libido. So big that I can't keep her satisfied. I'd have to fuck her 24/7. Anyway, she's had the waitress habit since day one, so it wouldn't be fair for me to suddenly start complaining.

I give the other two gals a nod as I slide into the water. Kerry does the same and puts her hand on my shoulder so they'll know we're together. We talk a little about how hot it is, how odd it is to see so many dykes at a Best Western off Route 66, and other chit-chatty stuff. Susan—that's the femme's name—hands me a joint. I take a hit and hand it over to her girlfriend, whose name is Dana. Dana tokes up and passes it on, and soon the four of us are happily making plans to head to the Grand Canyon together tomorrow.

I lean my head back and close my eyes, and Dana takes the opportunity to push her foot between my thighs. I hear kissing sounds and low moans. When I pick my head up to investigate I see Kerry and Susan entwined. My girl has a way of getting parties started.

Dana kinda looks like a surfer boy; I think this to myself as she pushes me against the side of the tub.

"We should probably go somewhere more private," she says.

I disengage just long enough to announce, "There's a king-size bed in our room."

I'm excited by the beauty of her body as I watch her walk across the parking lot. She's far bigger than I'd normally go for, the muscles I mean, and Kerry looks dwarfed as she walks alongside her.

In the parking lot, the freckly waitress catches up to our happy little band. Must be six o'clock. She hollers, "Hey, ladies, wait up," so I sprint up the burning cement stairs and throw open the door to our room. Five sweaty dykes tumble in and fall on the bed, quickly shedding four wet bathing suits and one polyester uniform.

The waitress flops right onto her back in the middle of the bed, and Susan, without so much as an introduction, dives between her freckly, tanned thighs. I hear her moan, "Mmm, wet pussy." And that's the last I see of her face for the next ten minutes.

I jump on the bed and stroke the freckly face of the waitress. She looks so happy. Before Kerry and I started this journey we call our relationship, I was living a suburban nightmare. My partner and I hadn't had sex in nearly a year. Before bed I used to hum, "Love will keep us together," Captain and Tennille style, to keep from mooning over the dull ache between my legs. And then this sexy dyke named Kerry parked an ugly yellow Dodge van in front of the bookstore where I spent eight hours a day. She waltzed into my life in thrift-store threads and long stringy rock-star hair and showed me a whole lot of sex and drugs. It's just like love, but better.

Kerry and Dana kneel at the edge of the bed and watch in admiration. But I want them to join us. "Get off your lazy asses and come over here and help us," I yell at them.

Kerry jumps up first and pushes me over onto my stomach, but I'm having none of it, so I shrug her off and push Susan out of the way and dive face-first into Freckles's damp musky wetness. Her pussy is inviting: hair neatly trimmed, big plump lips and a swollen clit to nibble on. She groans loudly as I pry apart her inner lips with the tip of my tongue. Behind me someone pushes against my ass, but I don't want to break the rhythm to see who it is, so I try to guess.

From between creamy waitress thighs, I say, "Dana, that must be you." But no one answers. Whoever it is makes a beeline for my ass and strokes my butthole with insistent fingertips.

I feel the fingertips pull away as Dana gets pushed down on the bed next to me. Kerry spreads Dana's legs and slips a couple of fingers into the woman's audibly wet cunt. "Can you take more?" she says.

Dana practically growls, "I can take whatever you can dish out."

"All right then." Kerry reaches straight for her G-spot. Dana arches her back and groans as Kerry pushes harder.

"Oh, yeah, fuck me," she says. "Fuck that hole, hurt it, break it."

And Kerry does. She pumps her fingers in and out, and the energy that those two create momentarily stops the rest of us. Dana yells so loudly even the waitress looks up. "Oh shit, oh shit, oh shit," she says. "Oh fuck, oh God."

"Aw hell yeah," says Susan as she takes Dana's place behind me. The thing that drives me nuts is ass-fucking, and Susan can tell, so she goes at my ass like there is no tomorrow and I can feel the tension building.

"Please," I say. And then, it's happening. Like something blossoming between my legs. Pure pleasure. I'm so happy at this moment. I'm always happy when I come.

I roll over and press my sweaty forehead to Dana's abdomen and laugh out loud at the bed full of naked dykes. "I never got this much action in San Francisco. Thank God for *Damron*."

Freckles sits up, pushes her sweaty hair away from her forehead, and says, "Do you think I'm waiting tables at Bob's Big Boy for the tips?"

FINALLY

Nina Parker

I spent most of my life wishing I could live down my good-girl image. I was always the one who looked like an angel, and no one suspected I wasn't. Not that I was so bad, but I couldn't seem to be bad enough to change anyone's mind. My pranks in high school and college didn't do it. I never got caught, and everyone thought I was a nice girl.

Then I hit my forties and life took a decided turn. Call it a midlife crisis if you want, but I started to feel really wicked and wanton. Maybe it was the hormones surging through my system. Maybe it was the alcohol. Who knows? It all started with a drunken kiss, mainly to get rid of an obnoxious bartender, but it turned into something much bigger.

It was girls' night out at work, and while most of my co-workers were straight, we had a few lesbians in the group. I was one of the few not in a regular relationship or married. We were celebrating Karen's approaching fortieth birthday. I was past that milestone already and knew it was both momentous and irrelevant. We ate dinner at a local restaurant, sitting at the bar rather than at a table and having a rowdy time. The bartender enjoyed the banter and kept us well supplied with drinks. As the evening progressed, the conversation grew more and more intimate—and profane.

"Are you horny all the time?" someone asked. The group agreed that we thought about sex all the time.

"I haven't been this interested in sex since I was seventeen," I admitted.

"What about your husbands? Do they get with the program?" Julie was one of the straight, single ones.

"Well, he says he likes it, but half the time he's asleep in front of the TV when I want to fuck," Eleanor replied with a sigh, drawing lots of knowing laughs. She had been married for a long time.

"Have you had an affair yet?" A few shook their heads vigorously, but there were several looks.

"I've been thinking about it," Amy confessed. "I met someone on the Internet and we've been sending each other some pretty hot emails."

"Have you met in person yet? Isn't that dangerous?" Dana asked. She was the most cautious member of the group. "Aren't you worried about getting some terrible disease?"

"You should forget the men and just fuck each other," I suggested.

Karen, who was married, laughed out loud. "No one would suspect a thing when we get together for coffee," she said.

I didn't think any of the straight women were interested in other women, but it was an intriguing idea. I hadn't been in a relationship for a while, and I was tired of picking up women in bars. It might be fun to play with someone I knew and felt relaxed with.

Later, when most of the women had gone home, Karen and I sat together over our drinks. The bartender leaned toward us and asked if he could make us something special. We agreed, then went back to our conversation. A few minutes later he set an obnoxiously pink concoction in front of each of us.

"What is it?" I asked.

"A Bartender's Kiss," he told me, leering at both of us.

It was awful: pink and frothy and too sweet. We each took a sip, thanked him, and proceeded to ignore the drinks and him. But he wasn't put off that easily. He kept coming back and making suggestive remarks. That's when I decided to do something.

Leaning toward Karen during a lull in our conversation, I put my hand on the back of her head and drew her toward me. The kiss was deep and warm and soft, ending with a bit of tongue. I'd meant it almost as a joke, but by the end there was something hot lurking behind that kiss, waiting for a chance to come out.

We broke off, laughing, and I glanced at the bartender. He beat a hasty retreat to the end of the bar and left us alone. The tension between Karen and me was great enough that we quickly settled the bill and headed for my car. I was giving her a ride home, being less drunk than she was. In fact, I was quite sober after our kiss. It had sucked all the fog from my head and left behind a single clear thought: I wanted to seduce her.

During the drive to her house, I couldn't stand it anymore and pulled over on a quiet, dark side street. Putting the car in park, I unbuckled my seatbelt and turned toward her.

"What is it? Is something wrong?" she asked.

"No, nothing, except I need to do this again."

I leaned toward her and drew her into my arms, my lips finding hers. The kiss was more urgent this time, my tongue searching her mouth for its opposite. I wasn't worried she'd push me away, but I hadn't expected her response. Her tongue met mine in a sinuous embrace that lasted a long time. With my arm wrapped around her waist, I slid one hand up her rib cage to cup her breast. It was full and heavy in my palm. She moaned into my mouth and lay back against the seat as I continued to kiss and caress her. Finally we broke off, both a bit breathless, and I started the car again. The rest of the drive home was quiet. We made some small talk but didn't discuss what had just happened.

The following weekend, Karen and her husband came over to my house for dinner. After the meal, I suggested we go out and sit in my hot tub. Since it was unplanned, they hadn't brought suits. Despite our small-town location, my deck was quite private and we all decided to go without.

Karen sat facing me, with her husband between us, looking up at the stars. Well, they were both looking up; I was looking at Karen's tits. They floated in front of me, glowing in the moonlight, and I wanted to reach out and touch them. Our legs were entwined in the dark water, and I stroked her calf with my foot but didn't do anything else for fear of discovery in our close quarters. It was exciting thinking about her body as we sat naked together, with her husband nearby and oblivious to my interest.

As they were leaving that night, I drew Karen aside into a long hug, my hand pressing against her lower back.

"Can I have coffee with you tomorrow?" I whispered into her ear.

"That would be great. Come over about ten o'clock," she replied.

She and her husband drove off, and I stood in the dark, my pussy throbbing.

The next morning, I spent more time than usual in the shower, shaving and grooming. I stroked my wet pussy lips, thinking about Karen, but went no further. I wanted to save my passion for her.

As I drove to her house, I thought about what was going to happen. From what she had told me, I knew she had been faithful to her husband but was feeling frustrated lately. I didn't know if she had ever been with another woman, though, and I was a little unsure how she would respond to my advances. Karen answered the door with a cigarette in one hand and a cup of coffee in the other. Walking past her into the hall, I reached out and took the cigarette away.

"I don't like the taste of cigarettes in the morning," I said, kissing her quickly. I walked into the kitchen and put it out. She poured me a cup of coffee, and I stroked her arm as she handed me the mug. When she bent down to get the cream out of the fridge, I ran a hand over her round ass. I felt her jump under my fingers. As she stood up, I pulled her to me, hands sliding into her back pockets, and kissed her again.

"I see you have more than coffee on your mind," Karen said. She smiled as we separated.

"Oh, yeah. Much more." I followed her into the living room and sat next to her on the sofa. I took a sip of my coffee and set the mug aside. She was looking at me over the rim of her cup.

"I've been wanting to touch these since you showed them off last night," I said, caressing her breasts with both hands.

"I didn't know you were that interested," she said casually.

"I couldn't very well make my interest known, could I?" I laughed.

"Bartenders are one thing, husbands another."

"Well, there's no one here but us."

Karen leaned back and set her cup down. I took that as an invitation and pulled her T-shirt up. She wasn't wearing a bra. Her nipples were large, a deep rose against the pale skin of her breasts. My fingertips circled them, making the skin crinkle and darken as her nipples hardened. I leaned down and took one in my mouth.

She moaned and shifted in her seat as I sucked the entire areola into my mouth, my tongue teasing the tip. I moved to the other breast, sucking it between my teeth as my fingers twisted the first one. Karen reached down and pulled her shirt over her head as I continued to explore her delicate skin. Sliding off the sofa, I knelt between her legs, my thumbs finding her nipples again as I gazed up into her face. She smiled down at me dreamily.

"Now for the rest," I told her.

My hands slid down her rib cage to her waist before slipping into the waistband of her jeans. She shifted her hips again as I unbuttoned the fly and drew her jeans down to her ankles. Her black thong peeked between her thighs as I pressed open her legs and kissed her from knee to groin. My fingers danced over the tiny triangle of the thong before slipping under the sides and drawing it down her.

Now that she was naked, I wanted to feel her body under me, my breasts pressing against hers, my pussy grinding into hers. I pushed her sideways on the couch and climbed up to lie on top of her.

"You have too many clothes on," she said.

Her hands ran up my back and under my shirt. She unfastened my bra as I kissed her throat, and then she drew shirt and bra over my head and off.

Skin against skin. Hot and silky soft. Our hands roamed over each other's flesh, my nipples hardening as they slipped against hers. I reached a hand between our bellies and found the hair curling over her mound.

"God, that feels so good," she whispered as my fingers found her wetness and slipped between the swollen folds of flesh.

I pushed first one finger and then another into her before drawing them out to spread her juices across her skin. "You taste so great," I whispered, bringing my fingers to my mouth and licking off her juices. I squirmed down between her legs, spreading them wide as I buried my face in the mass of curls. My tongue made a path down between folds of skin and back up. Pressing my fingers back into her pussy, I slowly searched for her clit with my tongue. It was a hard nub under my mouth. She squirmed and moaned, her hands in my hair now, directing me without words.

I slid fingers in and out, faster and harder, pressing up into her soft flesh with each stroke, toward her G-spot. I sucked her clit into my mouth, tonguing it gently at first then more firmly as her encouragements grew more vocal.

"Yes, omigod, there," she said. "Don't stop."

I wasn't about to. Her juices flowed down my wrist and chin as I reveled in her ripeness, her soft melon-scented flesh. Her orgasm, when it came, was delightful, rippling down her stomach and over my hand and into my mouth. I felt like I was eating it, swallowing it whole. It felt so good to be doing this with her. When it was done, I slipped my wet hand out of her and reached up to trace her lips. She tasted herself on my fingers as I stretched out beside her on the couch.

"That was amazing. I haven't come like that in a long time." She thanked me with a kiss.

"I think we should meet for coffee again." I laughed as I reached for my mug.

Not long after that, Karen's husband was transferred to Germany with his company, and she left me before we got another chance to meet. But I think about her from time to time and know that at least with her, I got to be the bad girl I always wanted to be.

TAG TEAM

Wendy Stevens

My girlfriend, Sarah, doesn't like people to know how much of a slut she is—even me. For a while when we were first dating, she put up a front like she simply wanted a little kissing, a little biting, some basic fucking, and that was it. She'd arch her back and come and grin and kiss me all over. She was passionate, using her whole body to seduce me, kissing me from the very top of my head down to my heels, but I felt something was missing. Finally, one day while I had three fingers deep inside her, I stopped. "Please, baby, keep going," she moaned, rocking her hips back and forth to try to get me to continue.

"Not just yet," I said calmly, looking at my pale, freckled, redheaded goddess. I kept my fingers inside her but simply held them still, trying to figure out exactly what made her naughty little mind tick. "I want to know what else you want," I told her. I didn't like the idea that my own girlfriend, the love of my life, was holding back.

"I want you," she cooed plaintively, ever the good girl.

"I know," I said, my fingers lightly trailing along her cheek, then her neck, before going in for the kill. I entwined them in her curly red hair and pulled, watching as her neck arched upward. I did that a few more times and wiggled my fingers inside her cunt, then pressed my short nails against the back of her neck. "But what else do you want? You'd better tell me if you want me to keep fucking you," I warned her.

Keeping my fingers safely inside her, I rolled her over, hoping maybe by not facing me she'd be better able to tell me what she wanted. My fingers played along her sweaty neck then dove again along her face, and her tongue reached out to lick me. I let her wet each finger, and then I stuck two in her mouth. She suckled them, holding on for dear life as I once again moved my fingers in and out, feeling her clamp around me. I started to match the rhythm of both hands, pushing into her mouth and cunt at once then easing out. Then I stopped again. "Really, Sar, what do you want? In your wildest fantasies. And I know you've got some."

A strangled cry escaped her mouth, her lips clamping down against my fingers as I spread my fingers inside her wetness. I pulled both hands out and waited. "What was that?"

Her words were quiet, and I had to strain to hear. "I want two cocks at once—yours and someone else's. I want you both to be mostly dressed, and me between you, one of you fucking me and one of you making me suck you off. I want you to use me like a toy," she said quietly, and I felt a few tears drip down her cheek onto my hand. I brushed them away then rubbed her clit in a slow, hard circle with my thumb.

"You mean you want one of us to invade that pretty little mouth, and one of us to fuck you right here?" I asked as I again shoved my fingers inside both of her holes.

"Yes," she cried out, her voice loud, and her body's reaction told me this was precisely the key to her hidden treasure. My mind immediately presented me with the perfect person to complete our rendezvous. My friend Terry is black, butch, and totally kinky. In real life, she's as mellow as they come, though she likes to fool people by rarely smiling, wearing camouflage, and raking her eyes over you in a way that makes you think she'd be a great cop, getting criminals to confess to crimes they haven't even committed. But Terry's charm is that once you break the ice and get past her stony exterior, she's sweet as pie. I think she likes being the tough badass on the street and a pushover in private. But there's another place where her badass streak comes out, and that's in bed. I only knew what she'd told me, but she'd told me a lot, and from what I knew, she'd love nothing more than to pound my girl's sweet pussy over and over while Sarah begged for mercy—and for more.

I didn't want to move too quickly. It was the middle of July, and Sarah's birthday was coming up in September. When I broached the subject with Terry, her eyes took on a sadistic gleam. "Your Sarah? You and me? As long as you're cool with it, Wendy, I'd be more than willing to fulfill her little fantasy."

With that arranged, my only other job was keeping my plans a secret from Sarah. The weeks seemed to fly by, and then finally it was the evening of her birthday. I'd told her she could go shopping during the day but to be back by eight, giving Terry and me time to get ready.

In our room, I proudly stepped into the harness, holding on to the fat purple cock, my own mouth watering with anticipation. I knew my sweet Sarah was about to go absolutely wild, to buck and moan and drool and maybe even cry when she got precisely what she'd been dreaming about for so long. When I'd adjusted my new cock exactly into place, I went about finishing my preparations; pulling on tight black jeans, a sturdy black bra, and a black T-shirt with the arms cut out.

I was making a cup of coffee when the doorbell rang. Terry came in and even I was amazed. She looked incredible, her hair shorn to perfection, wearing her favorite camouflage pants, loose white tank top that still managed to show her nipple piercings, and black combat boots. She cupped her crotch and gave me a knowing wink, and we switched from coffee to Bloody Marys, the warmth of the drink filling our veins. The scene about to unfold was perfect because although I thought Terry was hot, I didn't really want to have sex with her myself. This way I'd get to, but by proxy.

When Sarah finally came bustling through the door, she was crackling with energy, her cheeks rosy from the wind. When she saw Terry and me in the kitchen, calmly sipping our drinks, I could tell she had no idea what to think. She dropped her shopping bags in the hallway and shut the front door behind her. A few strands of her red hair caught in her mouth, and I put down my drink and came toward her, brushing them aside and giving her a long, deep kiss. "Hi, baby. Happy birthday," I said into her ear. She melted against me, her body curving deliciously into mine. "We're gonna celebrate your big day, just the three of us."

"Wha—?" she started to ask, then looked from me to Terry and back again.

"Whatever you're thinking, you're right," I said, and she just looked up at me with her big hazel eyes. "Why don't you go into the bedroom and show us what you bought today?" I was pretty sure she wouldn't have been able to resist the sale at the little lingerie boutique she'd told me about earlier.

I went back to the kitchen, where Terry let out a whistle. "Damn, girl, your woman really is fine as can be. I can't wait to get my hands—and other things—on her," she said, and suddenly I couldn't either. I gulped down the rest of my drink and went into the living room. I heard Sarah emerge, and when I looked up, she was wearing a sheer black nightie and the tiniest black thong imaginable, her bare toes painted with red polish. She wore just a little lip gloss, and all five feet of her appeared absolutely delicious.

"You look beautiful, Sarah," Terry said when she got near us. The room was filled with tension, both sexual and the regular kind. Terry had met Sarah at plenty of parties, but she'd never seen her practically naked, and I liked that all of us were turned on and slightly unsettled at the same time.

"Baby, why don't you tell Terry what you've been telling me? What your fantasy is? Here, I'll help you out." I stepped closer to her, fondling her breasts and feeling her nipples immediately harden. Her eyes widened, staring back at me, and I just nodded, giving her permission to go with what she truly wanted. Terry moved behind Sarah to massage her back, and when Sarah tumbled forward, pressing against me, I knew Terry must have pushed close enough to rub her cock against Sarah's backside.

I pulled on Sarah's nipples, letting my knee thrust between her legs, and her head arched backward, falling against Terry's shoulder. They made a beautiful contrast, with Sarah's ultrapale skin and Terry's deep chocolate-colored flesh, and any awkwardness quickly melted as Sarah struggled to articulate exactly what she wanted. "I want you both. I want you to tag-team me. I want to be between you both, sucking a cock while one of you fucks me," she said, the words half mumbled into Terry's neck but still intelligible. I ground my knee harder against her as I tugged her nipples, and when I felt Terry's hand nudge my knee, I moved aside to let her fondle Sarah's sleek entrance too.

I heard Terry undo her pants, and, I knew she was rubbing her naked cock against Sarah. "You mean you want me to fuck you with this, while you're on your hands and knees sucking your girlfriend's dick? Is that what you want, you little slut?" Terry hissed out the last words as Sarah thrashed between us as much as she could. I let go of her nipples and lightly caressed her neck, and that brief brush of my fingers made her cry out.

"Yes, yes. That's what I want," she said, and we both stepped away. Then, one of each of our hands on her back, we guided her into the bedroom and onto the bed. Sarah looked so beautifully brave; I saw doubt suddenly sneak up on her at times, but Terry and I were both quick to reassure her. I eased my purple dick out of my pants, guiding it through one of the buttons of my jeans so I was still fully dressed. At that sight, Sarah quickly forgot whatever qualms she might have had. While I knelt, my hands behind me against the headboard, she began sucking me. No sooner had her pink lips wrapped around the purple toy than I heard a loud slap and saw Terry had pulled apart Sarah's asscheeks, holding them open so she could view her tiny asshole and hold open her pussy lips. Terry's own cock was a fat blue one, and her face was tight with concentration and arousal, her eyes fixed downward, as she let it rub against Sarah's wet lips.

My girl gulped my cock mightily, her mouth straining as she took more and more in, and I could tell the moment Terry entered her, because she almost gagged, her throat opening up as her cunt was split open, plundered by Terry's invading dick. Sarah slid off my cock and let out little moans—"Uh, uh, uh"— that I recognized well.

Terry was holding on to Sarah's hips, for balance and to keep herself solidly inside. Sarah's body formed an S: her head held up to suck me off, her back arching downward so her slight belly undulated near the sheets, her ass arched high above her.

The sight was beautiful, and Sarah was clearly getting everything she'd wanted and more. I grabbed her by the back of her hair and guided her along my dick while I felt my clit swell and my own cunt ache to be filled.

"You like being the center of attention, don't you, birthday girl?" I said, tugging her hair by the roots as she swirled her tongue around my cock, making sure not to miss and inch. Terry was working a fast, steady rhythm, her hips bucking forward and back, sliding the blue dildo in and out of Sarah's juicy pussy. Part of me longed to see for myself the mix of colors, of wet and solid, of flesh and silicone, but I liked the way her lips were moving way too much to pause.

Sarah moaned, trying to talk, but the words simply slipped around the edges of the cock in her mouth and all that came out were garbled noises as she took the entire length of the cock. I felt the pressure of her mouth as she worked her magic, and even more, I felt something being released as she freed herself to enjoy this very special gift. I looked up at Terry's face, and she winked at me then moved her hands so she could squeeze Sarah's cheeks once more, this time while riding her, using her ass much the way I'd used her hair to guide her body for maximum pleasure. Sarah undulated, her body rippling as she accommodated both of us perfectly.

"That's it, you dirty girl, take my huge cock," Terry said, her voice guttural as she sped up, clearly racing toward her own climax. I suddenly wanted something else, and I pushed Sarah's face gently aside. I yanked open my pants and pushed them down, then got rid of the harness.

I moved closer so that Sarah could plant her tongue directly on my pussy. I needed to feel her, and see her, directly on my body. She zeroed in on my clit, just the way I like it, and then, without even asking me, she slipped the dildo from the harness where I'd dropped it next to her, and began fucking me with the toy. Her tongue was still circling my clit, pressing against my sensitive nub while I gripped the headboard hard for balance. Now I was the one threatening to lose control. When Terry saw what we were up to, she moved faster, the slurping noises of her cock in Sarah's pussy ringing loudly, almost as loudly as my cries when Sarah shoved the entire dildo inside me while nipping at my clit with her teeth. I'd already been teetering on the edge, and her forceful movements, practically demanding that I come, pushed me over. I felt like I'd been the one tag-teamed, and in a way, between her mouth and the toy, I had. I shuddered powerfully as I came, then slowly sank into the bed, cradling Sarah's face.

Terry bent over Sarah's back and fucked her hard. Sarah held on to me, her arms wide around my hips as Terry's cock took her again and again, until finally Terry let out a satisfied groan. She pulled out and then finished Sarah off with a few quick twists of her fingers, making my girl cry out against my thigh.

I said at the beginning that Sarah doesn't like people to know how much of a slut she is, but that's starting to change. The inevitable lesbian grapevine has made the story of our little threesome legendary, and I catch women winking at Sarah knowingly when we go to the local bar. She eats it right up, winking back and clutching my arm. Getting double-fucked is still her favorite thing to talk about in bed, and she's even suggested she might be able to take something in her ass next time around. However, we've decided to save this for a special occasion, like Sarah's next birthday. Which gives us almost an entire year of preparation—lucky me. Or rather, lucky us.

MY LESBIAN SEX CONFESSION

Teresa

It all happened during the August bank holiday in 1999.

Claire and I had been bumping into each other and giving each other a good licking and fisting every now and again since the day we'd left school. But sometime around May that year, ideas about fantasy role-play and being the naughty little schoolgirl punished by the strict headmistress had started to creep into our conversations, and the relationship had become more and more intense.

With one of us wearing our old school uniform and the other dressed in a sharp, stern skirt suit, we'd act out our student-teacher fucking fantasies on each other over and over again. But the one thing we really wanted seemed impossible.

We both wanted to be schoolgirls again and to be punished and abused by a gorgeous blonde teacher, just as we had wanted to be when we were at school and were being punished for our "disgusting and disgraceful behavior."

Finally, after much hard work on Claire's part, our fantasy was coming true. Someone would be visiting us at her house over the long weekend.

Claire had been planning it for a month but had refused to say anything about our visitor. In fact, I didn't even know if it was a man or a woman! I tried to get her to tell me, but she wouldn't crack. All I knew was that Claire was horny as hell at the thought of this person's visit and that she couldn't wait for the day to arrive. She grinned like a Cheshire cat whenever I mentioned it, and when we fucked I swear her honey had never tasted sweeter.

Eventually the big day came and I arrived in the afternoon with a bag of my school uniforms and plenty of knickers. I had packed some normal clothes as well but when Claire saw them she said that I shouldn't have bothered since we'd be schoolgirls all weekend.

Taking me by the hand, Claire took me upstairs and told me to change into my uniform. Eager to find out what was going to happen, I did so as fast as I could.

My pussy was dripping and my breath was quickening as I slipped into my lovely, new, white-cotton panties. And although I loved all this horny anticipation, it was almost a shame when they were ruined less than a minute after I put them on.

I was also watching Claire as she got changed into her pleated blue PE skirt, blouse, tie, white kneesocks, and black shoes.

My heart started to pound in my chest. It was really true. We were both going to be schoolgirls again.

Even while we both stood side by side in front of the dressing-table mirror putting our hair up in pigtails she refused to tell me what was happening. She just stood there grinning, telling me, "You'll find out soon enough."

Through the thin cotton of her blouse, I saw how hard her

nipples were. She stood with her legs tightly crossed, squeezing her pussy with her thighs. She was obviously very excited about something, and it was getting closer and closer with every tick of the clock.

I pleaded with her to tell me, but she just giggled like a twelve-year-old and led me back downstairs. Once we were there, we sat cuddled up together on the sofa staring at the clock, so horny that we both felt like we'd explode.

Claire was finally starting to crack under the pressure, but she'd only tell me the person would be here at seven o'clock and that if we weren't both behaving like good girls when she arrived, she would be very angry indeed.

At least I knew now we were expecting a woman. But how long would I have to wait before I could lick her out?

Of course, knowing we had to be good girls was like a red rag to a bull, because the only thing better than being naughty was being punished when we were caught.

Claire was the one who started it.

Licking her lips she put her hand between my thighs and stroked my pussy through my damp cotton knickers. Groaning with satisfaction, I reached out and caressed her firm, ripe tits through the cloth of her blouse. In less than a minute we were hopelessly lost in each other's arms and fucking like a couple of bitches in heat.

By the time the clock struck seven we were both a total mess. When someone finally knocked at the door we leapt to our feet with shock.

Claire and I pulled up our knickers and rushed to answer it. We stood side by side, smiling sweetly with our blouses unbuttoned and lipstick smeared everywhere our mouths had been. As soon we opened the door and I saw the face of our new teacher, I realized what Claire had been so horny about.

Standing angrily on the doorstep and towering over us in four-inch stilettos was Claire's friend Paula, a woman I will call Miss Johnson and worship until the day I die.

She wore a stern, charcoal-gray skirt suit with lapels so crisp you could cut your hand on them. Her shoulder-length hair was pulled into a tight bun with not a single strand out of place. As she sized us up with her steely cold eyes peering over the tops of her glasses, her expression truly frightened me, but it excited me too.

Claire and I curtseyed to her, lifting the hems of our tiny pleated skirts to reveal our moist shaven pussies. I didn't dare make eye contact. Even before she had said a word, I was in a submissive and cowering state of mind because she was so domineering she didn't even have to try!

Miss Johnson didn't even say hello. She was obviously disgusted with our appearance, which was just what we'd both wanted. Tutting with repugnance, she held out her car keys and told us to run out and fetch her bags.

At least twenty neighbors would be able to see us if we did what we were told. But having waited for months, we were both so horny we honestly didn't care. So without a second thought, we both muttered, "Yes, Miss," and curtseyed as we left.

After putting the bags upstairs in the room Claire had prepared for her, we stood patiently in front of Miss Johnson with our hands behind our backs waiting for her to punish us for our slovenly appearance—after the result of our little fuck on the settee.

We stood fidgeting with shame for what felt like minutes as she paced up and down before us, until finally she spoke. As she lovingly straightened our ties and smoothed down our hair, she asked in a soothing voice what we had been up to.

I told her we had been cleaning the house for her, but she was still curious how our lipstick had become so smeared and why we were such a mess.

We stood as we always had as schoolgirls, hands behind the back and feet apart. She put her hands up our skirts, pulled off our knickers, and groped our juicy pussies. Though she knew what we'd been up to and how horny we must have been, I really think she was shocked to feel just how juicy our pussies actually were.

Fuming and disgusted, she called us lesbian sluts and pulled us one at a time over her knee on the sofa and spanked our bottoms bright pink. As Miss Johnson spanked me, I actually came so hard I sprayed honey all over her hand.

Standing us side by side again, while tears welled in our eyes and we rubbed our sore bottoms, she shoved her fingers up our cunts and asked repeatedly if we were slutty lesbians and if we enjoyed being fisted by her.

Claire and I did our best to deny it as we gasped and wailed, our knees trembling as we grabbed hold of her wrists for dear life, but being fucked so roughly by such a dominant and intimidating figure eventually compelled us to talk.

I must have come twice before Claire finally gave in and confessed. I can tell you now, though, that when Miss Johnson had finished with us, her suit sleeves were soaked with our juices.

I was really quite sad it had ended so soon. It was one of the deepest, most intense, most satisfying fucks I'd ever had. But although the fisting was over, the fucking had just begun.

For the rest of the day Claire and I took turns having our bums and pussies caned, strapped, and paddled. She commanded us to kiss each other and suck each other's tits and eat each other out. Miss Johnson said she was trying to "beat our perverse tendencies out of us," and it was exactly what we had been longing for.

The thing I remember most is being forced to sit on Claire's old school desk with my legs apart as Claire bent over and touched her toes, buried her face in my pussy, and licked me out while her backside was being caned—until we were ordered to swap places.

It must have been three A.M. before we finished. We'd come so much that we'd stained the carpet, and our asses and palms were red raw. Even then, we were forced to assist Miss Johnson as she changed into her nightie and got into bed, and then to cuddle up at her feet.

As soon as we were sure she had gone to sleep, being careful not to wake her, Claire and I fucked each other stupid until the sun came up.

We were Miss Johnson's slaves all Saturday and Sunday. It was just like being on punishment back at boarding school, except for the relentless fucking.

Reporting promptly at nine in our neat uniforms, with perfect hair and makeup, we spent all day cooking, cleaning, and doing any other menial task Miss Johnson could think of.

Of course, she'd always stand behind us with a cane or a strap in her hand, ready to punish us for any slight misdeed, and we always did our best to make sure she had plenty of reasons to do so.

Only in the evening did Miss Johnson relax and unwind. Taking off her knickers, she forced us to take turns, one licking out her pussy as she watched TV or listened to music while the other stood holding her drink tray and feeling Miss Johnson's hand up her skirt.

She stripped and bathed us together both nights, paying close attention to our tits and pussies and turning a blind eye when we felt each other up. She would then towel us dry, slip us into the two, long, girlie white nighties she had brought especially to make us feel like schoolgirls, before brushing our hair and tucking us both into Claire's double bed, before getting ready for bed herself and going to sleep in the guest room.

We were all far too horny to sleep, however, so each night at about three A.M. she would perform a dorm check, and woe befall us if we were doing anything we shouldn't be.

Dressed in a sexy black nightie, dressing gown, and slippers, Miss Johnson quietly crept into our dorm room, flashlight in hand, and reached up underneath our bedclothes to check the state of our pussies, which were dripping, our having fucked each other stupid since "lights out."

Claire and I pretended to be asleep the whole time as, throwing off the bedclothes, she knelt between us and slipped her fingers one by one up our juicy cunts.

"Wake up, darlings," she whispered. "Auntie Paula wants to talk to you."

I thought my look of shock and surprise was really rather well acted as I woke up to "suddenly" find my teacher on my bed with her fist inside my pussy, but Claire insisted that I hammed it up far too much.

Once we were awake, Miss Johnson proceeded to make sure we wouldn't be up to any more filthy behavior by making sure we had come at least five times so that we were either satisfied or just too knackered to do anything when she left.

I still vividly remember lying on the bed as Miss Johnson sat on my face, her thighs holding me securely, and urged me to lick harder. At the same time I heard her hand slap against soft flesh and Claire whimper with pain and delight.

At the end of Sunday's dorm inspection, she gave us each a good hard fucking with the flashlight, slapping our asses and shouting at us to "take it like a woman" until we collapsed on the bed weeping tears of exhaustion and relief.

It was absolutely wonderful, but we knew the following day would be her last.

On Monday morning we arrived promptly for inspection to find her standing with her car keys in her hand. She had decided we were going into the city for the day, and there was nothing we could do to change her mind.

Claire told me later that my jaw dropped so far that Miss Johnson could have fit the car in my open mouth. Going out in public in a tiny pleated skirt, white knickers, and kneesocks? She had to be joking! Then Miss Johnson said something about it being all right as it was a bank holiday and there were bound to be fewer people around. The next thing I knew, Claire and I were in the backseat of her car being driven to the shopping mall in Newcastle, a place I'd never been before nor have I been since.

For the rest of the day we were dragged around all the shops that were open. But while Miss Johnson seemed very relaxed, I spent most of the time pulling my skirt hem down as far as I could and feeling people's stares all over me.

It was obvious Claire felt the same, but we were betting Miss Johnson would have no problem making a scene, or perhaps even punishing us in public, so we kept up the act.

Miss Johnson had it all worked out. If anyone asked—and a few did—she was a teacher from a boarding school outside town and as a reward for our good conduct she was taking us shopping.

It was the most humiliating experience of my life, but I can't help getting wet thinking about it. I was dripping like a tap then too, and when we stopped at the big seating area surrounded by cafés and restaurants, I'm sure I must have left a puddle on the plastic seat.

Miss Johnson had all the money—we didn't even have any

pockets—so she went over and ordered a coffee and Garibaldi for herself, and two Pepsis and sticky buns for us.

When I had finished, with the icing from my bun all over my fingers, she took me by the hand and walked me to the toilet, complaining for all to hear about what a mess I was and how she couldn't take me anywhere, before pushing me into a stall, pulling off my knickers, sitting me down on the toilet, and giving me the deepest, most satisfying fist fuck of my life.

Lifting her skirt to reveal that she didn't have any knickers on either, Miss Johnson pushed my face into her cunt and ordered me to eat her out. The danger of getting caught made it so good you wouldn't believe it.

Having smartened back up, I was led back out and made to sit alone while she obliged Claire in the same way. Then we walked to the parking garage where Miss Johnson said her good-byes.

She had packed her bags the night before and discreetly placed them in the trunk. Only when she got in the car and started the engine did reality kick in.

She was going to drive off without us!

"How the fuck are we going to get home?" I screamed after her.

"Hitchhike!" she yelled out the window. That was the last word she ever said to me, because to this day I haven't seen her since.

For the next hour, with no money, no cell phone, and no way of getting home, Claire and I hung around the parking garage not knowing what the hell to do. When a nice older woman came and asked if we were all right, convinced we were lost schoolgirls, we both played along and did our best not to touch each other's pussies as she kindly drove us home.

Despite being left in the garage like that, however, we were both so horny when we got back to Claire's house that we spent the rest of the day in her bed reliving the whole experience. Even though I don't see Claire anymore, I think about this little adventure often, and it makes me wet every time.

TOY STORY

Daisy Lopez

"Wanna hang out at my place after work?" Talia asked.

"Yeah, sure, whatever," I replied, handing a cute guy his change. He smiled at me, sort of stroked my fingers as I dumped the coins into his hand.

Talia rolled her eyes and shouted, "Next!"

I'd been working at the gas station/restaurant for about a month, and despite our obvious differences, Talia and I had really hit it off. She's a funky sort of Goth/punk girl, skinny, with long, straight black hair and real pale skin. She has a stud in her nose and a broken-heart tattoo on her left shoulder. Her dark eyes are rimmed with enough liner to make Ashlee Simpson jealous. I'm a bit of a girlie girl, petite, with shoulder-length blonde hair, green eyes, and what my mom calls "an utterly adorable smile."

Talia normally worked the front cash register and pumped gas while I waited tables in the restaurant. I was earning extra spending money for college in the fall. Talia was working full-time to support herself.

"What's the address again?" I asked, when we'd hopped in my car at quitting time. The gas station was way on the outskirts of town. Talia normally took the bus to and from work.

"Just drive, Daisy," she said. "I'll steer you in the right direction."

I giggled. My dad would've had a fit if he'd seen me hanging around with a girl like Talia. I started the car up, and she punched on the radio. Hilary Duff came tinkling over the speakers.

Talia stuck a finger in her throat and pretended to barf. "You listen to this shit?"

Blushing, I checked both ways for traffic before pulling out onto the highway. "Uh...sometimes," I mumbled, as Talia laughed.

She fiddled around with the radio until she got a heavy-metal station then amped it up so loud I thought my head would explode. It didn't, and half an hour later I pulled up in front of a row of townhouses in a kind of crummy area of town. "Looks nice," I said.

"Looks like shit," Talia said. She pointed a purple fingernail at the last townhouse in line. "I live in number six."

I glanced around at the rusty cars lining the street and the group of skuzzy guys hanging around the convenience store on the corner. "Um, maybe I'd better be getting home, Talia. I have to—"

"C'mon," she interrupted, turning off the car and pulling the key out of the ignition. "Don't go chickenshit on me. There's some stuff I wanna show you."

I followed her into the house. It wasn't too bad, I guess, but it was awfully small. "Are your parents at work?" I asked.

Talia tossed me my car keys, then shut and bolted the door.

"I just live with my mom. She's at work, yeah. She's got the night shift at the hospital. Want a beer?"

I shook my head, and Talia grinned. She grabbed my hand and pulled me into a bedroom. "There's some stuff I wanna show you," she said again.

I sat on the edge of the bed while she pulled a box out from underneath it—a box full of magazines. She threw one at me. "Take a look at that shit," she said.

I caught the magazine and stared at the glossy front cover. It showed a photo of two naked women, a blonde and a brunette, their tongues touching and their big boobs pressed together. The magazine was called *Lesbian Lickers*.

"Uh...huh," I said, feeling kind of scared. I put the magazine down next to me.

"Weird, huh?" Talia said, plopping onto the bed and picking up the dirty magazine. "Think maybe my mom has gone lezzy or somethin'? She hasn't had a date with a guy since Dad dumped her, like, two years ago."

Talia scooched closer, and her leg touched mine. We were still both in our uniforms—mine a tan blouse and skirt, Talia's a blouse and pair of jeans. She flipped the magazine open. The dark-haired woman was licking and sucking and biting the blonde's big pink nipples in a series of pictures on one page, sticking her tongue right in the other woman's spread-open pink cunny on the next. My face got all red and my hands damp.

"Crazy, huh?" Talia said. "And take a look at this."

She dropped the open magazine in my lap and clicked on the TV that stood in a corner of the room, the DVD player on top of it. The screen filled up with a naked blonde and brunette. Yup, the same two from the magazine. The blonde was sprawled out on her back on a bed, the brunette working a pink dildo in and out of her cunt.

"My mom's gotta be a lez, huh, Daisy?" Talia said.

I swallowed real hard, my eyes shifting back and forth between the magazine and the TV. I hadn't seen so much porno since Mom and I spring-cleaned my older brother's room one time. "Um, I—I don't know," I mumbled. "Maybe your mother is just, you know, curious or whatever—experimenting." I sounded really dumb, but that's what you sound like when you're tongue's all thick and stuff.

Talia laughed. "C'mon, Dais, she's forty-five, for Christ's sake. She's not eighteen like you and me."

I was shaking a little, feeling the warmth of Talia's leg against my bare skin, feasting my eyes on all that porno, listening to all the rude things the brunette woman was saying to the blonde. I just about jumped out of my skin when Talia suddenly put her arm around my shoulder.

She stared into my eyes and breathed, "You ever get curious, Daisy?"

I gulped. Talia rubbed my bare arm and my body got all hot and tingly, a little lightning bolt shooting through my pussy. "Um, uh, well, I—"

She kissed me, all soft and warm and a little wet, right on the lips. I felt like I was melting. When she pulled her head back, I sat there like a love-struck dweeb, my eyes and mouth half-open.

Talia laughed, like it didn't mean anything. She pushed me away and jumped to her feet. "Take a look at this other shit I found," she said.

I almost fell off the bed, but I held on to the magazine. Talia rummaged around in the closet and dragged out another box. I kept one eye on her and one on the TV. The blonde was squeezing her big boobs and twisting her head from side to side, thrashing around on the bed and moaning and groaning while her girlfriend pumped her with the pink dildo and licked at her clit.

Talia pulled a pink dildo out of the box and waved it under my nose.

"There's all kinds of dildos and vibrators and junk like that in here," she said.

I nodded vaguely. Talia dropped onto the bed and playfully pushed the tip of the dildo against my lips. I opened up my big mouth and kind of sucked on the pink plastic. And that changed everything. Suddenly everything got all serious. I got real scared then—scared and excited, actually—realizing what I'd done, what I'd never done before.

I mean, I'd practice-kissed with a couple of girlfriends before—you know, getting ready for the big moment with boys—but that was all just giggly, girlie, innocent stuff. I'd never, ever gone seriously lezzy with a girl before. Never even really thought about it. But now, with those two beautiful women going at it right in front of me, and with beautiful Talia breathing down my neck, I wanted to experiment—right now!

I stared openly into Talia's dark, sparkling eyes, and she fed more of the dildo into my mouth. I sort of bobbed my head back and forth on it like I was sucking a guy's dick. Then Talia pulled the dildo out of my mouth, all wet and glistening, and stuck it in hers.

I could hardly breathe. She put her arm around my shoulder again. She slid the dildo out of her mouth, swirled her pink tongue all around it, then slid it back into my mouth. I kind of quivered with excitement, feeling the incredible heat of the girl, her softness; my pussy was so damp and squishy I thought I would wet the bed.

Talia glanced at the TV, and I followed her eyes, still sucking on the dildo. We both watched what the brunette was doing to the whimpering blonde with her pink dildo. Then Talia shoved me back on the bed. She pushed my skirt up to my tummy, exposing my soaked panties, and I knew what she was going to do to me.

I held my breath, the blood pounding in my ears. Talia pushed my legs apart and touched my panty-covered cunt with the dildo. "Yes!" I yelped, my body jumping. Shaking all over, I grabbed the bedspread.

Talia rubbed the dildo against my electrified pussy, sending blazing sparks all through me, setting me on fire, turning me wetter and juicier than I'd ever been. Then she slipped a hand inside my blouse and grabbed on to one of my titties.

"Fuck, yes!" I hollered.

Talia grinned at me. She expertly popped my bra open at the front, covered one of my naked boobies with her warm hand, and squeezed. I absolutely flooded with joy. I bit my lip and squeezed my eyes shut and let the wicked heat wash all over me. Over and over, Talia stroked my pantied coochie with the dildo, groping my boobs and rolling my blossomed buds between her fingers. I took it and loved it, shivering with delight.

"I'm...I'm gonna come, Talia!" I wailed.

"Nope, not yet you aren't," she said. She pulled her hand out of my blouse, and the dildo away from my smoldering pussy.

I scrambled up onto my elbows and squirmed higher onto the bed as Talia gripped my sodden, heart-patterned panties on either side and yanked them down my legs. My face burned even brighter when I felt the warm air and Talia's eyes on my exposed coochie. My blonde fur was all shiny with moisture, my lips red and puffy with excitement.

Talia tossed my panties aside, then climbed on the bed and touched my bare pussy with the dildo. I jumped. The blonde on TV hissed, "Fuck me!" at her girlfriend, and I hissed, "Fuck me!" at Talia.

She plunged the dildo into my slit.

"Oh, my God!" I squealed.

Talia shoved the dildo all the way into my steaming cunt. And that cocky pink thing was at least ten inches long! I almost squirted right then and there, but I managed to control myself—barely. Talia eased the dildo out of my slit then plunged it all the way back in again. She pumped me ferociously, grabbing one of my boobs and really pounding my slit.

I stared at her, all wild-eyed, my body rocking back and forth, my head spinning, my pussy buzzing with a warm, wet sensation I'd never gotten going solo. The blonde on TV suddenly screamed at the top of her lungs, her body jerking, girl juice actually jetting out of her cunny and into her lover's face.

I trembled, out of control, a way-serious tingling building up in my pussy, pumping higher and higher with every stroke of the dildo. Talia fucked me faster, pulled on my buds. When she lowered her head and licked at my clit, it was too much for me.

"Mmmm, yes!" I shrieked, tensing then exploding. A humungous orgasm went off in my dildo-stuffed cunny and crashed through me. Quickly followed by a second—and then a third!

I gushed hot juice all over Talia's flying hand, onto her outstretched tongue, shaking like she'd Tasered my pussy. I totally lost it for a solid minute or so, fucked to the most awesome ecstasy ever by my wicked girlfriend Talia.

I don't know if I passed out or what, but it seemed like a long, long time later that I felt someone kissing me—kissing my boobs, nibbling on my nips. My eyes flickered open. It was Talia.

I pushed myself up onto my elbows, and my head spun and I saw stars. I was groggy, still glowing with the warmth of multiple orgasms. I licked my lips and was about to thank Talia for the truly wonderful experience when she said, "My turn."

I tried to focus, to figure out just what she meant. Things got a whole lot clearer when she stood up, took off her blouse, and peeled off her jeans. The girl didn't believe in underwear—she was totally naked!

I blinked my eyes and stared at Talia's skinny bod. Her titties were way smaller than mine, barely more than two bumps and a pair of cherry-red nipples. But those nipples were something, long and hard and pointing straight at me. Her coochie was completely shaved bare, her lips pouty and slick looking. She had a silver barbell in her bellybutton and a black butterfly tattooed on her lower tummy.

"Um, what do you want me...?"

Talia pointed at the TV. The porno movie was, amazingly, still going, the blonde giving it to the brunette from behind with a strap-on dildo.

I gulped. Talia grinned. Then the crazy chick lifted a black belt with a big red dildo attached to it out of the box of goodies next to the bed. I'd never even seen a strap-on in person before, let alone knew how to use one. Talia showed me.

She pulled me off the bed and fastened the belts around my hips and bum, the bright, red dildo sticking out ludicrously from my cunny. It felt weird wearing that thing, and a little loose. Talia cinched me tighter, and the dildo part pressed firmly against my pussy. Then she dropped to her knees and started sucking on the foot-long cock.

"Yeah, um...suck me," I mumbled, totally unsure of myself. I grabbed on to Talia's shiny hair and pulled her head closer.

She liked that. "Make me suck you off, bitch!" she hissed, staring up at me.

I jerked her head forward, and she gagged on the dildo, coughing and spluttering when I quickly pushed her head back. She attacked the dildo again, and I yanked her head forward again, forcing her to swallow my cock.

I planted my feet and gritted my teeth and held her there, her cheeks bulging, her eyes watering and nose running. When I finally pushed her head back, she gulped and choked, the dildo popping out of her mouth all drippy and slimy with spit.

She sucked me some more as I watched the women on TV, how the blonde gripped her girlfriend's waist and pumped her hips, pumped the brunette. My cunny got all tingly with the sight of those sexy women and the friction of the strap-on rubbing me the right way as Talia sucked.

I pulled the girl's head up. "I'm gonna fuck you!" I growled, sounding all tough and experienced. I hadn't even had full-on sex with a guy yet, for God's sake, let alone with a girl.

Talia jumped to her feet and kissed me, stuck her tongue in my mouth and swirled it around. I got all warm and fuzzy, and I tried to grab her and lick her back, but she wriggled out of my hands and dove onto the bed. She got up on all fours and shook her skinny butt at me, daring me to do her.

I followed her onto the bed, my prick bouncing up and down like it had a life of its own. I kneed in behind her, put my hands on her bum, then stopped and tried to catch my breath. It was totally nuts—sweet little Daddy's girl Daisy getting ready to screw another girl with a strap-on dildo while hard-core lesbian porno played in the background. It was wild and crazy and absolutely wicked, and I went for it.

I gripped Big Red and shoved the tip of it into Talia's glistening cunt lips. I had to kind of feel around for her hole for a second, but I found it. When I did, Talia impatiently shoved back, burying the plastic prick to the hilt inside her.

The impact of her slamming ass-backward against me sort of stunned me, rocked my pussy and my brain. Her smooth skin was hot against mine, and I could smell her dripping pussy. The strap-on moved against my own pussy as Talia wiggled her ass, and I got all damp and dizzy like before. Was I seriously going to have full-on sex with another girl? You bet I was! I moved my hips, sliding my cock back and forth in Talia's stretched-out slit.

"Yeah! Fuck me, bitch!" Talia yelled, twisting her head around and glaring at me.

I grabbed onto her waist like the woman in the movie and really pumped my hips. I got a smooth, fast rhythm going, slamming the plastic cock into Talia's pussy, her lips gripping the pistoning dildo, my thighs smacking loudly against her rippling buttcheeks.

"Harder! Faster!" she screamed.

I went as fast as I could, digging my fingernails into her flesh. The dildo flew back and forth in her hole, the bed creaking and banging the wall. Talia clawed at the bedspread, moaning, matching the ecstatic moans of the brunette on TV. Then she suddenly tensed up, muscles locking in her back and arms. I pounded her even harder, and she was jolted by orgasm.

"Fuck almighty!" she wailed, shuddering with ecstasy.

I kept right on fucking her—fucking her and fucking myself—the friction on my clit sending me sailing all over again. We came together, both of us blown away by the wet and wild ride.

It was when we were cleaning things up a bit that bad-girl Talia 'fessed up to the fact that she actually lived with her father, not her "lesbian" mother. The porno magazines and DVDs were his, the many sex toys hers.

THE SAILOR

Diana Cage

From the back she really looks like a sailor: Tight white pants. Broad shoulders. Short-cropped hair. The nape of her neck is bare and sexy. The uniform fits her very well, and I pretend for just a moment that she isn't dressed up in some very obvious costume at a party that feels like the fetish prom. From the front, she's very much a girl. Freckles, thin nose, high cheekbones defining a decidedly feminine face that I'd bet is the bane of her existence.

The room reeks of propane from the fire show. Earlier, two women danced around each other in a way that was supposed to be sexy. They swallowed huge, silicone cocks with flaming ends, made a big show of their tattooed bodies and pretended to fuck each other. They had everything going for them—beauty, style, even enthusiasm—but it was all too staged. They were too black and shiny and clean to be having real sex. They looked like a movie. Like some teenage witchcraft rip-off, straight-to-video bullshit. "Stop trying," I said out loud. "Put your rubbery clothes back on and go back to your co-ops." Even the girls on the dance floor, in their PVC outfits and bondage gear, looked bored. They need rape scenes or foot-fucking—murder and mayhem. Something spectacular to get them off. A little half-assed flaming-sword-swallowing doesn't get anything going for this crowd.

Girls are coughing from the thick greasy air. And a few have passed out on the dance floor like little latex canaries—only to be escorted from the building by EMTs who assure us they will be fine and tell the rest of us we need to go outside and get some air.

All the good beer is gone. The music is bad. I am feeling lightheaded and loose, and looking for trouble. For a moment, my sailor disappears from sight and I panic, thinking I won't get a second chance. But she resurfaces among a group of tranny boys, all huddled together away from the girlie-girls, like little kids at recess. Her beautiful face looks a little bit mean even though she's laughing. Looking at her makes me feel sexy, and I wonder what it will take to get a girl like that to fuck me. Then I remember that we all want to fuck someone.

The club I'm in is normally a gay men's porn theater. Live jack-off shows, the works. But tonight it's been rented out for a lesbian fetish party and latex-clad enema nurses are chatting with Catholic schoolgirls. I came with my girlfriend Steph, who likes these parties more than I do. She's having fun, chatting up the cute little boys and girls. All of our friends are here. Every once in a while she brings me a beer, pats my head, kisses me and then goes back to our circle of friends. Normally I'd join her, but tonight it's boring to me. Same people, same outfits. The beer helps some but not enough. I've just been hanging around the bar staring at everyone. I don't even feel like dancing.

I head outside and bum a smoke from a group of shrieking, silly girls in marabou boas. A gorgeous redhead in a pink plastic skirt offers me a cigarette, which I accept, but I decline her offer of a light. Instead I go looking for some solo leather-jacketed type with a well-worn Zippo. Hey, we all have our fantasies. The truth is, I don't even smoke. I just want something to wrap my lips around—something to keep my mouth and hands busy. When the sailor walks outside, my spirit lifts. She notices me standing there expectantly with unlit cigarette, and I feel a little obvious as I hold it up to be lit. We don't say anything. Up close she's even prettier. Blue eyes, black hair. I'm too tense to flirt with her so I just look down at my hands.

"Are you having fun?" she finally says to me as she holds her silver Zippo to my cigarette.

I grasp her hand to steady the flame and she winks at me in a gesture that's both boldly flirtatious and totally cheesy. "Not really," I answer.

"Seen it all before, huh?"

I can't tell if she's making fun of me, so I shrug and we stand there smoking in silence for a long moment. Then she stubs out her cigarette and walks back inside.

I feel a foreign sensation as she leaves. I can't place it. And then I recognize it as desire.

Her smug face, her perfect stance—all of it both pisses me off and makes me wet between the legs. I don't know what it is about attitude that can get my panties so in a knot. But give me a cool babe over a nice one any day. I crumble.

As I'm finishing my smoke, Steph walks outside looking for me. She offers me another smoke, so I take it. Still feeling warm and riled up, I study her face closely. *I can pick 'em*, I think. She's really gorgeous. Handsome is a better word, I guess. Her sandy-brown hair keeps falling into her eyes. She's so relaxed

and happy and sexy that I feel a twinge of guilt for taking her so
for granted. Then she puts her arm around me and protectively
walks me back through the door.

There's a stairwell to our right, and I have yet to explore it.
Suddenly I'm curious. "What's downstairs?" I ask her.

She says, "Private video booths where you can watch porn
and jack off, and rooms with curtains for anonymous sex."

"You're kidding," I say. And then I blush at how naïve I
must sound. Of course that's what's downstairs. I'm at a sex
party, in a porn theater. What the fuck did I think was down
there? Storytelling hour? She looks at me quizzically, trying
to gauge my interest in getting fucked before she says, "Okay,
babe. Let's go."

It's cooler downstairs. The air is fresher. And it's much quieter. Steph is holding my hand, playing tour guide. She's telling
me about the glory holes in the video booths but I only half hear
her. My thoughts are on the sailor. The way she lit my cigarette,
the way she looks from the back. The way she walked away
from me. I'm dimly aware that Steph is dragging me into one of
the booths.

"Let's watch some porn," she says. "Come on, baby." She
leads me in and shuts the door. "Don't worry, the doors lock."

How handy, I think.

She puts some quarters into the slot, and the TV lights up.
The boys on the screen are really young. Barely eighteen, I'd
guess. They're pretty and hairless, so I pretend they're cute
butch girls pretending to be fags. One girl is bent over a chair
getting fucked. She's moaning. Her cock is rock hard and she's
stroking the hell out of it. Steph slips her hand under my T-shirt
and pinches my nipple so hard I hiss. I feel the throb in my clit.

My cunt becomes a liquidy place, like my head.

Usually when Steph and I fuck, I think about her hand in my

cunt. I concentrate on the sensations, the rhythmic circling or the pounding, the feeling of her skin on my skin. I think about how happy she makes me. But on this particular night I can't concentrate. My mind is too cluttered. I imagine the young boys on the screen. Their asses, their hard cocks. I'm overstimulated. Steph's hand is working me, playing me. She knows how. She's so good. She knows just where to stroke and how hard. She's doing it so right. Just like she did it to me earlier, just like she'll do it to me later. But it's no good. I can't come. I'm not even close. "Come for me, baby," she whispers in my ear. "Show me how much you love me."

Frustrated, I turn away from her and face the wall. She follows me and pushes me down toward the small stool in the corner. I start to protest, not wanting to be on my knees on the floor of this booth where random guys have sucked random cocks, but I catch a glimpse of something through the glory hole that makes me change my mind. My sailor is in the next booth. She's leaning against the wall with her pants unzipped. She's not doing anything really, just staring at the screen with a blank expression. I position myself for a better view and this makes Steph happy because she has better access to my cunt. I feel her hand run down the crack of my ass before she pulls it back and smacks me hard. She does it again and this time I lean into it because it's something I can feel.

I can see my sailor clearly. She's staring intently at the screen. I wonder if she's watching the same two young boys I was looking at a few moments ago. The video is still playing. I can still hear them groaning. Her blue eyes are half-closed and her hair is a little messy, like she's run her fingers through it a few times and broken up her hair gel. She looks better this way. Hotter. Looser. Something.

She slips down her pants and briefs and slides a hand

between her legs. I watch her fingers disappear into the vertical folds of her cunt and reappear glistening over and over, making that slick *tic tic* sound. Her face is expressionless; she's just staring at the screen, jerking off in the most perfunctory of ways.

Steph is still fucking me, but suddenly I can feel her more than I did a few moments ago. A cloud has lifted, and now my swollen crotch demands attention. "Fuck me harder, baby, please," I say to her and she does, taking the opportunity to slide another finger in. She leans over me, presses her body against mine. Fingers buried to the hilt in my pussy, she nuzzles my neck with her teeth. I adore her so much. She's an amazing lover and a loving girlfriend, but right now I'm thinking about the stranger in the next booth and Steph's hands on my body.

Steph is really turned on. I can tell from the rough way she's pushing into me. It must be the porn working its magic on her. I'm hot too, and very close to coming, but I hold on for sailor boy's sake. When I feel Steph's thumb at the opening of my cunt, I gasp, ready to take her whole hand. I love it when she fucks me like this, so raw and so forceful. And the sensation of her pushing into me brings me back to where we are, and who she is and why I love her so much. "What are you thinking about, baby?" she says. "Where are you? Come back to me. I want to feel your cunt on my hand."

I can see sailor boy's hands moving faster over her clit, and I wish I could reach her with my tongue. I groan and push back against Steph shamelessly in a way I know she loves. My sailor's mouth is open. She flicks her clit a few more times and tenses up, pressing her fingers down into a pussy I didn't get to touch or taste. It's enough though, and it pushes me over the edge and I gasp as the wave of orgasm hits me.

Steph stops moving momentarily, her fingers still inside. The sweat that's collected between our bodies has dried and our skin is stuck together. "Don't move," she says to me, and I obey. We stay like that for a few moments, and when I look again, my sailor is gone.

THE PAYOFF

Lois Glenn

My mouth had a bad habit of getting me in trouble. That's why I found myself walking up the path to Shea's house with an overnight bag. I usually spent my weekends hiking around the surrounding mountains, discovering rarely used trails and communing with nature. It helped me to release the stress of the workweek, recharge for the next, and return prepared to handle the major and minor crises that invariably cropped up. This weekend would be different. This weekend I had to pay off a bet that should have been a sure thing.

It had started innocently enough. Shea and I were watching the Phoenix Mercury versus Houston Comets basketball game at Misty's, a lesbian bar on Indian School Road. She had been harassing me since the start of the WNBA season about how the Comets were going to wipe the floor up with the Mercury. It had been Swoopes this, the Comets that for two weeks. She had even sent me an e-gram with a comet crashing into the planet Mercury.

The planet had disintegrated, and in its place was Sheryl Swoopes moonwalking on top of Diana Taurasi's prone body.

I let her have her fun. Let's face it, the Mercury weren't what you'd call consistent. They were still a young team trying to find their legs. So when the Mercury were up by seventeen points at halftime, I thought I'd do a little razzing of my own. That's where all the trouble started.

"You think Van Chancellor is in the locker room reminding his players they're not on a cooking show?" I kept my eyes focused on the television set to hide the smirk I knew was on my face.

"Why do you say that?" Shea said. Out the corner of my eye, I saw her eyebrows furrow.

"They have more turnovers than Betty Crocker." I busted up laughing. I even slapped the bar to make sure she knew how funny my joke was.

"Oh, shuddup." Shea play-punched my arm. "It's obvious the refs are blind. They're calling the Comets for ticky-tack shit while the Mercury should be arrested for mugging."

"You're right." I nodded solemnly as if in agreement. "That's the first time I've seen a foul called for just plain sucking." I was laughing so hard I couldn't drink my beer for fear of choking.

"Just wait till the next half," Shea said with underlying faith. "They'll come back."

"Come back? First they got to show up." I laughed some more. "I think they're still at the mall shopping for shoes." I knew I was pushing it, but I couldn't help it. Since the inception of the WNBA, the Comets have been the bane of the Mercury's existence.

"You'll see." She took a sip from her beer. "Never count the Comets out."

"Diana Taurasi is going to get a hand cramp from writing all those thank-you notes to the Comets players," I laughed, feeling pretty sure about the outcome of the game. *"Dear Comets players, thank you very much for gifting us with this win, allowing us to jump ahead of you in the standings."* I mimed writing in the air above the bar. I should have stopped while I was ahead, but the beer was flowing and Shea had it coming after all the ribbing I'd endured the past two weeks.

"Care to make a wager?" She kept her eyes on the television set, which showed a commercial of a woman jumping on a mattress.

"A bet?" I couldn't understand why she'd want to make a bet when her team was down by almost twenty points at halftime.

"Sure." Shea glanced my way almost nonchalantly.

I reminded her of the obvious. "The Mercury *are* up by seventeen points."

"Then you shouldn't be worried." She sat there with her shit-eating grin, drinking her beer like it was her team up by seventeen.

"I don't know," I said, testing to see if she was serious. "It's not inconceivable for a team to come back."

"Well, if you're scared…" She drained her beer and waggled the empty bottle at the bartender to get her attention.

"No, it's just that seventeen points really isn't that bad." Although I was starting to question her sanity, I was also curious what the punch line was. "What are we betting?"

"Loser is the winner's slave for a weekend." She paid for the two beers Danni placed in front of us.

"Slave?" I glanced up at the TV again. The score was still thirty-seven to twenty, Mercury.

"Yeah." She grinned at me and winked.

What the hell? Now I was feeling very confused. She did know the score, right?

"Well, I don't want to be washing dishes and stuff all weekend," I told her. Even with her cockiness, I wasn't feeling nervous. I just wanted to see what her game was.

"Oh, so you're admitting the Comets will come back and kick the Mercury's asses?"

Damn, it figured she wouldn't bite. "No, I just think it's only fair you agree ahead of time what I'm allowed to make you do. I wouldn't want you to think I was taking advantage because your team had an off day." *That ought to shut her up*, I thought. I took a drink of my beer feeling smug.

"If I win you have to stay at my house for an entire weekend. That means Friday night till Monday morning." She laid her arm along the back of my stool and whispered in my ear, "And have sex any way I choose."

What the fuck? I choked as my beer went down the wrong pipe. "S-sex w-with y-you?" My inability to formulate words had nothing to do with the beer searing my lungs.

"Any way *I* choose." For a full minute I stared at her, speechless.

"But we're both...I mean you are...and I'm..." I was having a hard time figuring it out. I felt like two trains were colliding in my brain.

I considered us both butches, and sex with her wasn't something I'd ever contemplated. I mean, she was my best bud, not my girlfriend. We knew each other's fantasy women and what we wanted to do in those fantasies. We weren't supposed to think about each other in a sexual way. We were more likely to slug each other in the arm than hug. I took a big swig out of my beer, trying to picture it in my head. It didn't help. Damn it, this was Shea. We didn't even flirt. It just would not compute, and I was afraid I might fry what little brain cells I had if I continued to try to make sense out of it.

"What?" Shea seemed a little insulted. "I know I'm not all

femme like those bimbos who keep rejecting you, but I'm not butch either." Technically, that was true. Although she didn't wear dresses and makeup, she didn't wear jeans and muscle shirts like I did, preferring slacks and blouses. But damn it, she knew stuff, like the first time I tried to use a strap-on and I fell out the window. I thought that damn paramedic was going to have a heart attack, he was laughing so hard.

Mentally, I started to take a tally. She's five-six and can carry a hundred-pound bag of cement without breaking a sweat. She wears earrings, but they're usually shaped like dolphins or parrots, not those dainty pearl types. She knows how to change spark plugs. She likes to cook. She doesn't carry a purse, preferring a backpack. She likes babies. She knows who Brett Favre is. Her favorite color is purple. She didn't cry during *City of Angels*, but she did cry at her sister's wedding. We'd seen each other puke, for fuck sake. What the hell was I thinking?

"Boxers or briefs?" I asked, trying to think of anything that would make the picture clearer, not that I was really that worried about losing the bet. I just needed something to erase the butch-on-butch action from my short-circuiting mind.

"Commando." Even if she was teasing, that one word made my heart pound in my chest. Was she trying to kill me? What kind of power trip was she on? "You'd better decide fast. They're starting their warm-ups."

I glanced up at the monitor. The score was displayed prominently across the bottom of the screen. "Okay, but you're camping in the Superstitions with me," I said, referring to the mountains east of Apache Junction, famous for their Lost Dutchman's gold-mine legend. "I mean the *whole* weekend this time," I said pointedly. The one and only time Shea had agreed to go camping with me, she ended up crossing paths with a scorpion and refused to stay for even one night. It took me hours to decoupage her desk at work with photocopies of the definition for the word *camping* as my way of revenge. "And the whole slave thing still applies."

"Sex in the mountains sounds fun," she said. With her arm still along the back of my stool, she put out her hand. "It's a bet."

"Bet." I happily shook her hand before I realized what she'd said. *Huh? She doesn't mean...* I had no intention of having sex with Shea in the mountains or anywhere else. But I just let it go and turned my attention to the game, having every confidence in the world that the Mercury would hold their lead.

I should have known better. Never make a bet when you have no control over the outcome. Swoopes scored thirty-five points in the second half, and Taurasi couldn't buy a basket at the Wicker Barn. That night I cursed Diana Taurasi, Sheryl Swoopes, and the entire state of Texas as I rang the doorbell at Shea's home.

"Oh, I see you didn't chicken out." She was all smiles when she opened the door wearing a sleeveless white shirt untucked over brown cargo pants, sans shoes or socks.

"I never renege on a bet." I walked past her and tossed my bag on the floor next to the couch. "You gonna feed me first or are we gonna just rip each other's clothes off right here in the front room?"

Shea laughed. "Can't wait for me to sink my fist deep inside you, huh?"

She walked up behind me and wrapped her arms around my waist. I felt her breath on my cheek as she pulled me in tight against her body. Her hands roamed over me, alternately caressing and massaging. She began lightly touching the undersides of my breasts with the palms of her hands until my nipples stood erect. I found myself too lost in the pleasure of her touch to fight her for control. Then she squeezed each breast firmly, rubbing especially hard around each nipple. Her uncharacteristic actions caught me off guard almost as much as the sudden jolt of desire that shot through me.

"I just want to get started so we can end it." I'm pretty sure I said that without stuttering.

"Patience." She released her hold on me and walked down the hall to her bedroom while she spoke. "We have the whole weekend ahead of us."

I wasn't sure if I was supposed to follow her or not. I debated internally for a minute as I caught my breath and then started in that direction. She met me just outside the door to her bedroom.

"First things first." She held something out to me. "Remove all your clothes and put this on."

"You've got to be kidding." I stared incredulously at the Comets jersey bearing the number 22 she'd shoved into my hands.

"The only clothing you will be allowed for the entire weekend is this jersey." Her arrogant smirk was starting to annoy me.

"What? That's insane." I'd rather have leeches covering my body than wear the enemy's uniform.

"As my slave for the weekend, your main objective is to please me." She stepped closer to me. "You wearing this jersey and nothing else will please me immensely." In a very low, seductive purr, just mere inches from my ear, she said, "Don't you want to please me?"

Words fled from my mind as breath hissed from my lungs. What the fuck? Did she really mean *that* kind of slave? What. The. Fuck? Panic was screaming in my mind. I just thought we'd have sex then watch a movie or something. I wasn't expecting her to really go through with the whole slave/mistress thing.

"Your name for the weekend is Comet and you are not to speak without permission." As I stared at her with what I'm sure was a fish-out-of-water look, she managed to maneuver me into the bedroom. "Don't be long," she said as she left the room after giving me a slap on my ass.

I looked ridiculous, standing in front of the full-length mirror with nothing on but that jersey. What was this, a child's size? It was tight across my breasts and barely hung past my hips. My crotch was only half covered and my asscheeks hung out. My legs had never seen the sun or a razor. As I stood there in front of the mirror, I once again took the liberty to curse out Diana Taurasi, Sheryl Swoopes, and the state of Texas.

"Oh, Comet, dear, I'm waiting," Shea called in a singsong voice, interrupting the start of the very good mope I had going.

"This sucks." I took a deep breath to prepare myself for my humiliation and left the room.

"There you are." The smirk on her face told me she knew exactly what I was thinking about her little surprise costume. "I have a craving for a banana split," she said. "Gather the ingredients and take them out to the Arizona room." Without another word she left me to my task.

She hadn't told me to make her a banana split, just to gather the ingredients. With that in mind, I rummaged through her kitchen for the items. It appeared Shea had all the ingredients prepared and waiting. I listed each item aloud to help me remember everything. "Let's see, ice cream. Chocolate, vanilla, and strawberry." I took out the three separate gallon-size containers and stacked them on the counter. "Chopped walnuts, pineapples. Ew, don't like them." I left the crushed pineapple in the icebox. "Cherries, butterscotch topping, chocolate syrup, and whipped cream. Oh, bananas, can't forget them. That's the most important ingredient."

After I had all the items gathered, I wondered how I'd carry them all out to the room without making more than one trip. "Oh, yes." I spied the supply of plastic grocery bags stuffed inside another bag hanging on the wall. I managed to take everything out in one trip.

Shea was stretched out on a lounge chair watching me as I crossed the threshold. I was very self-conscious of my butt hanging out, but she never took her eyes off me. Turning my back to her, well aware she had an unobstructed view of my bare ass, I removed the items from the bags and placed them on the table.

"Name everything off as you place the items on the table," she said.

I rolled my eyes at her Cleopatra voice but did as instructed. When I laid the last item down, she asked, "No ice cream scoop? Were you planning on dishing it out with your hands?"

"Shit." The word was barely out of my mouth before I felt her body press into my back.

"I didn't give you permission to speak, Comet." Her hands grabbed my inner thighs and spread them as she pulled me into her body, causing me to lose balance. My hands slapped down on the table in an instinctive reaction to keep from falling. "Am I going to have to discipline you, already?" she said.

My nipples hardened as she bit my earlobe. I gasped, not from pain but from surprise at how my body responded to her touch. I was used to being the one in control and dictating the course of events. This wasn't the way I was used to being with anyone, much less Shea.

She released my earlobe. Her mouth kissed down my throat and licked my pulse point, which was beating erratically. One of her hands slid up my thigh to grasp my crotch. Her other hand traveled up my body to cup a breast. Her thumb rubbed circles over my nipple. I couldn't keep my breathing from escalating. I heard a groan, probably from me, but I hoped it was her.

Just when I thought she was going to slide her fingers through my wetness, she pulled her hand from my crotch and turned me to face her. Her hand twisted in my short brown hair and pulled my head back. As our gazes locked, I saw gold flecks dancing with desire in her brown eyes. Our lips were just inches away from each other. I waited anxiously for that first kiss, a kiss we had never shared, a kiss that would redefine our relationship forever.

"Take everything back to the kitchen and put it away," was all she said before releasing me and leaving the room.

"Fuck." I closed my eyes and tried to get my breathing under control. *Damn it, what's wrong with me?* I thought. *I'm a top.* Once I could open my eyes without getting dizzy, I placed everything back in the bags and returned the ingredients to their places in the kitchen.

I didn't know where she had disappeared to and wasn't sure what I was supposed to do next. Deciding I'd better find her, I started for the kitchen door. I'd only taken one step when she appeared. Gone were the white shirt and cargo pants, in their place a purple satin robe. Two thoughts crossed my mind as I looked at her. One: *Why did I ever think she was butch?* Two: *I never wanted to be a robe so bad in my life.*

Dark blonde hair cascaded around her strong tanned face. Her gaze caressed my body, causing me to tremble with an aching need I'd never felt before. In the two years I'd known this woman, I never once considered her as a possible lover, until this very moment. I truly must not have been paying very close attention.

"Take off that jersey," she said, her voice low and husky, like I imagined it would sound if she had just woken up. Glad to be rid of the offending thing, I almost ripped it as I struggled out of the tight piece of cloth. I vowed to never put myself in a position to betray my loyalties again. She snatched the jersey from me before I could toss it in the garbage.

"Don't add to your punishment," she stated matter-of-factly. She laid the jersey on the counter out of my reach. "Before the weekend is over I may require you to wear it again." I secretly hoped she'd find it preferable for me to go the whole weekend bare-ass naked. Hell, she'd already seen my entire body. No reason to cover up again now.

"Now it's time to address your breaking of the rules." Shea walked closer to me. In a panic I visually scanned her body for any apparent whips or floggers, taking a relieved breath when I realized her hands were empty. I started to worry again when I imagined what might be under her robe. She was close to me by the time my brain had gone through several scenarios, not alighting on a single one that put me back on top.

"Stand with your back against the counter," she commanded.

I did as instructed. A shiver trickled through me as my bare skin met the cool surface.

"Keep your hands where I place them." She grasped my wrists one at a time and raised them above my head. She pressed the backs of my hands against the cupboards hanging over the counter behind me. Satisfied with the placement of my upper extremities, she used her knee to spread my legs farther apart.

"Stay like that until I give you permission to move." She stuck her hand in the pocket of her robe and pulled out a blindfold. I was enveloped in darkness as she settled the blindfold over my eyes. "Do not make a noise and do not move."

I felt a chill across my body when she moved away. I stayed where she had left me, trying to guess where she was by the sounds. Although I couldn't see her, I felt her stripping away my every defense with her hidden gaze.

"Do you know how long I've wanted to fuck you?" she said.

I didn't answer. It had never crossed my mind that she did. I'd just assumed she felt the same way I did about our relationship. She was quickly proving how wrong I was.

"I'm going to stand here and look at you for a while."

My mind conjured up the picture of her looking at me standing spread open for her to see. I felt myself getting more excited.

"After this weekend," she said, "I may never get the chance again—might as well make the most of it."

It occurred to me that Shea might be feeling what I felt when looking at women, and it took all my willpower not to rip off the blindfold and reach for her. I was already wet from our previous encounter. I felt that wetness seep down my thighs the longer I stood with her invisible gaze burning through me.

"I expected you to have a tattoo. Don't all you badass biker women get tattoos to show off your toughness?" I wasn't sure if this was permission to speak, so I remained silent. "You may answer, Comet." I heard the amusement in her voice.

"Having a tattoo doesn't make you tough," I said, happy to note that there was hardly a quiver in my voice.

"I have a tattoo." I felt her step near me. "Are you saying I'm not tough?"

I didn't answer. Not because she hadn't given me permission but because my mind was busy trying to figure out what kind of tattoo she would have and where it might be on her body. Then the thought of her body made my pulse jump and lust clouded my mind.

"Answer me, Comet!" Her left hand reached between my legs and pressed into my mound. With her fingers spread wide, she used the heel of her hand to apply pressure, and while it was certainly pleasurable, I was unprepared for how my clit tingled in anticipation. My head fell back in bliss.

"Answer me," she ordered. She ground the heel of her hand

into my crotch. Electric shocks pulsed in my clit and my heart skipped a beat.

Shit, I had no idea what the question was.

She must have sensed my dilemma because she asked, "Do you think you're tougher than me?"

"Oh, hell, no." That was an easy question to answer but my words came out in a hiss of breath between clenched teeth. We had spent several drunken nights comparing childhoods. There was no doubt in my mind how tough she was.

"That's better," she said. Something, it might have been her finger, trailed down my skin from my collarbone to my left nipple. "I remember the first time I saw you." Her finger circled my nipple. "Do you remember?"

I did, but she didn't give me a chance to answer.

"I was playing softball. You were so busy trying to pick up that redhead, I doubt you even knew there was a game going on. I hit a line drive foul right into your solar plexus. You dropped like a limp noodle." Shea's hands roamed over my body as she spoke. The pain in my solar plexus that day was a distant memory next to the aching need I felt under Shea's touch. I wanted so badly to touch her. The only thing keeping me from moving was my determination not to show any weakness.

"You got your breath back, we went back to the game, and you went back to trying to pick up that woman." Something warm and wet enveloped my nipple. My brain identified it as Shea's mouth. I didn't need my sight to know she was sucking my nipple while her tongue flicked over the surface. My breath left my body, and my bones turned to jelly.

"Don't move." Her need-filled voice tickled my nipple, reminding me of the situation. With forced determination, I tried to find the strength to keep from crumbling to the floor. I felt her mouth slide across my chest to the other nipple. Each flick of her tongue sent a jolt straight to my clit. I was sure there was a small lake between my legs.

Shea released my nipple, and I felt her standing erect in front of me. I sensed her hands settling against the counter on either side of my waist as she leaned her body into mine. The whisper of her breath floated across my lips. "I'm not sure who was more surprised when I drove another foul into your solar plexus that day." I was having a hard time controlling my breathing as her robe-clad, hardened nipples rubbed against my painfully excited ones.

"When you got your breath back, you looked at the woman and said, 'A simple no would have sufficed.' I vowed right then and there we were going to be friends." The caress of what felt like downy soft feathers moved across my skin causing me to involuntarily shiver. I felt goose bumps rise in the wake of the contact.

My eyes blinked from the unexpected glare of light as the blindfold was removed. As my eyes focused, I took her in. A small smile played over Shea's lips, as if she could read the hunger I knew had to be showing in my eyes.

"Gather up the banana-split items and take them back out to the Arizona room. Don't forget the scoop, this time." She turned and walked out, leaving me trembling with raw desire.

Fuck a duck. She was driving me crazy with these fucking bump-n-goes. I pushed out a frustrated hiss of breath between my clenched teeth like wind across the desert.

I stood alone at the end of a uniquely designed lounge chair, taking in the changes to the Arizona room while awaiting further instructions. Lit candles bathed the room in an ethereal glow as Nusound's *Erotic Moods* CD played in the background. Padded extensions branched from the sides of the chair allowing a seated person to be restrained, completely open, and ready for her lover's pleasure.

"Lie faceup on the chair," Shea said as she entered the room, still clad in that purple robe. "Get comfortable. You'll be there a while."

Once I was settled, she replaced the blindfold over my eyes. She bound my ankles and wrists to the extensions and adjusted the chair back until I was almost parallel to the floor. Although the chair was comfortable, I felt exposed and vulnerable, knowing she had a clear view of my wet, throbbing clit. She held my breast in her hand, the nipple between her thumb and finger. My body arched as she applied pressure to my nipple. I clenched and unclenched my hands as a shock wave of pleasure coursed through me.

The next thing I knew, my breasts were coated with cold fire. "Vanilla and strawberry on the breasts. Chocolate down below." As she sucked the ice cream from my skin, the combination of cold and warm moisture rocked me to the core. I tugged at the restraints, desperately trying to get closer. Wetness pooled between my legs. I needed to feel her everywhere at once. I became lost to the world as each touch of her tongue and mouth sent shivers of pleasure all through my body.

I was so close to exploding that it took all my self-control to keep from breaking her no-talking rule by begging her to fuck me. Gasping for air, I tried unsuccessfully to guide her teasing lips to my quivering clit to give me a much-needed release. She kept me on the brink, not giving in to my nonverbal pleas.

The doorbell chimed repeatedly, breaking through the heady mist of my arousal. Shea feathered my lips with kisses, and I savored the taste of her blending with strawberry and chocolate.

"Be right back." She walked away, leaving me teetering on the edge of orgasmic insanity.

F-f-u-u-c-c-k-k, she's trying to kill me. I strained to hear what was going on in the other room. The sound of more than one pair of footsteps approaching made me feel more vulnerable than I'd ever felt in my life. By now, however, I was so crazy with lust-filled need I couldn't care less if a whole convent's worth of nuns had arrived, as long as they'd cool the fiery sensations searing through me.

"I invited some friends over to join me in some celebratory ice cream," Shea said when she returned. I tried to interpret how many "some" meant.

"You might as well undress now," Shea told her guests. "The ice cream melts fast and you'll just get messy." Fingers pinched my left nipple, and I arched into the contact. "They'll be coming off eventually anyway." This comment induced mild laughter followed by the rustling of clothing. It wasn't long before I was able to determine that there were now three mouths feasting on my body.

"I think this banana is frozen." That sounded like Janet, a beautiful woman with long blonde hair and a nice tight ass. If Janet was here, Sam was too. I should have known they would be the ones Shea had called. Sam and Janet had known Shea for years. She had even stood up for Sam at their commitment ceremony.

"Hmm, I wonder how we can warm it up?" Janet said. "Oh, I know." A cold hardness slid into my hot wet passage. "Mmm, how does that feel?" Despite the coldness moving within the pulsating pressure between my legs, my body burned like molten lava.

"Oh, careful." Shea's voice contained amused caution.

"Oops, it broke off," Janet giggled, as I felt what I guessed was the banana remaining motionless inside me.

"Guess someone's going to have to suck it out." Sam's desire-filled voice sent a shiver through me. Damn, what was it with me and butches today?

"Sam," Shea said in a playful warning tone, "this is my celebration. I get first taste." Her tongue touched my clit, and I could no longer think in complete sentences. My leg muscles clenched and unclenched with the pleasure. I tried to be quiet because she hadn't given me permission to make noise, but I just couldn't hold back the moans.

"I'll just try out the whipped cream then," Sam said.

The unmistakable sound of whipped cream being squirted from the can added to my sensual pleasure. From the sudden chill, I could identify the parts Sam was interested in feasting on.

"Can't forget the cherries," Shea said.

I couldn't tell where the cherries were placed. I did, however, feel a warm, wet tongue scoop into my belly button as lips sucked around the outer edge. A trail of wet kisses traveled from my stomach to my breasts where lips sucked hungrily. At the same time, another pair of lips followed the same trail, until I had a pair of lips feasting on each of my nipples.

Meanwhile, Shea buried her face between my legs, emitting small sounds of pleasure. I moaned as she pulled my folds apart and stuck her tongue deep inside me. Her tongue and lips moved the softening banana in and out several times before extracting it for good with a combination of sucking and licking. Shea's teasing lips explored the most intimate regions of my body, sending waves of pleasure pouring from my hot center into her mouth.

Janet had abandoned my breast to straddle my head, facing the length of my body. Taking a deep breath to immerse my senses in her scent, I kissed up her firm thighs until I reached her clit. A small gasp escaped her when my lips touched her wet folds and she stretched out prone down my body.

As her tongue joined Shea's in an intimate dance entwined with my clit, I switched from kissing to licking her sweet wetness, slowly yet firmly swirling my tongue across her folds. I wanted to tease her and make her orgasm build to the most explosive she'd ever had by mouth.

"Hell, Janet, you know how that turns me on." Sam's husky voice was thick with need. "I've got to fuck you." Before long what had to be a latex cock brushed against my lips and tongue as it slid deep into Janet's sweet opening. Sam slid the dildo in and out, faster and faster, while Janet ground into my face. Sam's pelvis slapping into Janet's ass didn't hinder me in any way from licking and sucking Janet's sweet juices.

"Oh, yes, please, please." Janet stopped licking me long enough to plead with Sam, or me, or both. "Oh, please. Don't. Don't. Stop." Her words came in gasping breaths as she neared the edge of bliss. She pushed farther into my face giving me as much access as she could, while still keeping rhythm with Sam's thrusting. The intoxicating flavor of an excited woman danced across my tongue until Janet was screaming and pushing with everything she had against Sam's driving cock.

"Oh, yes. Oh, yes. Make me come. So good. So damn good. Oh, yes." Janet was gasping for air as her orgasm crashed through her like a tidal wave. My face and shoulders were wet when she was done. I absolutely love making another woman do this.

At the same time, Shea's tongue dove deeper and deeper into my wetness causing me to buck uncontrollably. I wanted—needed—her to put out my growing fire. A chorus of slurping and groaning echoed around the room as an explosion of white lights blasted behind my covered eyelids. The most intense orgasm I'd ever felt sent my soul orbiting out of control.

"Want to see who's been feasting on you?" The blindfold was removed, and I blinked my eyes to bring Shea, Sam, and Janet's forms into focus. "What fun is winning if your friends aren't there to join in the celebration?" Shea chuckled, looking quite pleased.

All three of the women unbuckled my restraints, as I lay gasping in a sweaty, sticky mass of limpness, trying to regain my strength. I noticed the strap-on proudly bobbing between Sam's legs. Her dark hair brushed against her shirt collar as her hazel eyes watched me, a knowing smirk on her face.

If I survive this weekend, the first thing I'm going to do is check the schedule for the next Comets/Mercury game, I thought, as Shea gave her crew cleanup instructions.

GOING FISHING

Cheri Crystal

I hadn't seen Gerri since the night before she left for Women's Week. The fact that I missed her after only a week was starting to scare me. I was falling for her, and only a concrete floor could stop me. She'd flown to Provincetown with a couple of friends from work, and I was supremely jealous that they'd gone without me. It was impossible to get the time off from my job no matter how hard I tried to finagle it, and besides, I hadn't been there long enough to rate a vacation. I'd driven Gerri to the airport and given what I hoped was an Academy Award–winning performance of being okay with her departure.

Gerri and I worked together, and even though it was against company policy to have sex with a coworker, regardless of gender, I had the hots for her. I'd heard rumors from reliable sources that she had a history of breaking hearts. As much as I didn't want to top the long list or lose my job I couldn't control my feelings any more than I could control the tingle in my clit whenever she was around. I was happy when she took me up on my offer of a ride home from the airport, since we'd be able to spend some time together outside of work.

At the end of the week, I eagerly went to pick her up. It was a good thing her plane landed on time since I arrived at the airport an hour early. When I spotted her approaching, I was delighted to see that she was alone. It turned out the other two women had opted to stay in Provincetown a few extra days—lucky them, or more accurately, lucky me. As Gerri walked toward me, I saw that her ruddy complexion was simply radiant, accentuating her dazzling bright blue eyes. There was a roughness to her angled features, from years of playing outdoors, that had captivated me from the moment I'd set eyes on her. I noticed her cheeks were red, maybe even a bit chafed.

I longed to run my fingers through her short-cropped blonde hair. It looked windblown and messy, just the way I liked it. I impulsively hugged her as she shifted the backpack to her other shoulder. Seemingly unfazed by my overly friendly gesture—we weren't on a hugging basis—she flashed me her best "Gerri" smile and winked. I melted.

Weak at the knees and barely recovering, I asked, "How was your trip?"

"Great," she said, and we started walking to baggage claim.

We made our way to the luggage carousel and waited. I took in how tight her jeans were and was envious of the intimacy the material had with her crotch. When she noticed the direction of my gaze, she gave me a knowing look. I averted my eyes and blushed, but I couldn't look away for long. I was drawn not only by the tight jeans showing off her long trim legs but by the way her jacket barely reached the top of her butt. And what an amazing butt she had. She was still talking when I realized I'd missed most of her conversation since I was too busy mentally undressing her. My hungry gaze traveled north and lingered on her breasts. I imagined she wasn't wearing a bra and her small firm breasts needed to be tweaked.

"I heard it rained," I said as lights flashed, a buzzer sounded, and the conveyor belt was activated.

"The sea was full of fish, and the town was full of lesbians. I didn't notice the weather. Did it rain?"

"Very funny." I grinned up at her feeling like a lovesick fool. She was at least a head taller than me even with my two-inch heels. Glancing at a candy wrapper on the floor, I was certain I had a dopey look on my face.

"P-town was fantastic," she said. "First the fish—I caught three blue fins and one striped bass from the breakwater and one striped bass from Herring Beach. The weather wasn't ideal for sunbathing, but I fished and loved it." Her animation whenever she spoke of her fishing expeditions was adorable. Not missing a beat, she saw her suitcase and grabbed it off the conveyer belt with ease. "Just need the fishing-rod case and we're outta here."

As it made its way down the belt, we spotted the four-foot tube with her prized possession; it was impossible to miss. I offered to take it, but she almost bit my head off.

"Nope. Nobody touches the rod case."

"Okay." I put my hands up in surrender and backed away but only slightly. *She sure is touchy about that fishing rod, isn't she?* I thought. "I could take the other bag then."

"Got it," she said forcefully.

Did she think she'd have her butch card revoked if she let me help? I already knew how strong she was from watching her single-handedly rearrange the storeroom at work or move the massive copy machine when something fell behind it. Nothing was too heavy for her. She could probably pick me up while carrying a ton of bricks with one hand tied behind her back, even if I wasn't five foot two and 110 pounds soaking wet. How I longed for her to try. *Am I getting too carried away here?* I thought. *I wish!*

Once she had the suitcase, rod case, and backpack securely in her grasp, we made our way out of the building. It was hard for me to keep up with her long-limbed pace. I'm sure I had to take three steps for every one of hers. *Breathless* was a good word for how I was feeling, but it wasn't entirely due to walking so fast.

"I love being out by the sea," Gerri told me. "That's one of the reasons I fish. Catching them is a bonus. I'd never live far from the coast. I reckon I'd pine away," she said.

"Sounds wonderful. Take me with you next time," I said.

She stopped for a second and looked directly at me. "You want to fish with me?" I nodded and hoped I didn't appear too eager. "Wow, you're the first woman who's asked to fish with me." She seemed genuinely surprised.

"I like to fish," I said, trying to lure her in with my seductive tone.

She must have missed it since she kept on walking as we made our way out of the terminal. The cool October night air did nothing to dispel my heat.

"Mostly I ask women to come along and they don't turn up."

"I find that hard to believe. Who'd ever stand you up?"

"You'd be surprised." She stopped just two inches short of colliding with a skycap, and I watched as she ran her fingers through her hair.

I stopped to face her while she waited for the man to move the luggage rack. "Well, *I* wouldn't." I don't know if it was the way I said it or the way I looked at her, but she finally had my number. Surprised, she fixed me with a gaze that felt like a microwave heating me to the core. My face felt like it was on fire, matching the heat starting in my belly and radiating right to my clit.

"Easy girl! You're not flirting with me, are you? I'll treat you bad if you are." Gerri cocked her eyebrow and I thought I would die. "Don't start me up or I may get rough with you."

"Promises, promises," I replied a bit more boldly.

"Oh, so you like it rough?" Was she daring me?

"Oh, yes, the rougher the better."

My tits stood on end as I wished with all my heart that she would ravish me right then and there. I would kneel at her feet submissively if I had to, but she didn't have to know that.

"Careful, you may just get what you wish for."

"You don't scare me," I said bravely, while the thought of what she was capable of doing to me had me wet. *Are you daring her?* I asked myself. *Yep!* I thought, smiling inwardly as we walked to my SUV. Fumbling with my keys, my hands visibly shaking, I barely got the door open before she threw in her bags and pressed me up against the cold metal, pushing the door closed beneath my trembling body. Her arms and legs had me pinned to the passenger-side door. Shock yielded to surprise when her mouth came down hard on mine. I could barely breathe, but I had more important things on my mind.

Before I knew what had hit me she had her callused hands on my taut nipples. The rough skin of her palm sent shivers down my spine and into my pelvis. Gasping for breath, I tightened my arms around her waist and parted my lips for her to penetrate me with her tongue, deepening our kiss.

Fueled by a longing I had nursed for months, I was insatiable for her touch. I reached toward her chest, but she intercepted my hands. She wouldn't let me touch her breasts, and I cried in protest. She silenced me with another kiss, and my breath caught. Her hands moved to the top of my jeans. I nearly fainted, but she held me up with her thigh between my legs.

Before I knew it, I was sprawled out on the backseat of my SUV and she was ripping off my boots and then my jeans. I rarely wear underwear since I hate panty lines and thongs. I purposely didn't have any on, and the effect of her discovery was evident on her lust-filled face.

We were in a public lot, and although it was late, there was still the chance other people could be lurking about looking for their cars. The thought of being caught with my pants off and my legs spread open for the whole world to see excited me to no end.

"You like it rough? Well, that's what you're gonna get," Gerri said.

I felt her thrust two fingers in and out of my wet, inviting cunt. I gasped when she added two more fingers. She was pounding me, my hips keeping a perfect rhythm like a choreographed dance. I wanted her—no, I needed her—to touch my clit, but she was too busy with my hole, teasing me, tormenting me. I tried to get her to touch my neglected nub, but she relentlessly avoided my need.

Finally, she thumbed my clit while finger-fucking me hard. I bit my lip. My breath was coming faster, and I grew closer just as she removed her thumb. *Shit! Don't stop.* Getting desperate, I shifted my hips, hoping my clit would come closer to her thumb, but it was to no avail. She was such a tease. I dripped with desire as I tried to nudge closer to her hand.

"Gerri, my clit...oh, please," I sobbed.

"You begging me?"

"Yes, I...please."

"Stop saying please. Just tell me what you want." She appeared to be enjoying her dominant butch status, but I saw right through her feigned irritation.

"All of you...in me." I needed her so bad I thought the world would crumble if she didn't take me completely right then.

She thumbed my clit once more, sending shock waves through my pelvis and tightening every muscle in the lower half of my body all the way down to my toes. Then, just as quickly, she removed her thumb. I groaned long and loud as she gave me an evil lopsided grin. She was so damn cute!

"You are such a fucking tease," I said and pulled her mouth once more to mine. I bit her lip then licked and kissed it.

Gerri put my right thigh over her shoulder and leaned into me, pressing her jeans—or was that her belt buckle?—into my clit. I was more open and desperate than before, especially when she went in for a firmer grasp on my tits.

"God, Ger. You trying to kill me here?"

"You wanted rough..."

"Yeah, rough. Fuck me hard. Plea—" I stopped myself from finishing, hoping I'd get what I wanted. I was so wet, so turned on, so in love, I surrendered to her, and she could have whatever she wanted from me at that moment.

Before I knew it, her whole fist was inside me, and I was crying out in ecstasy. "Yes," was all I could manage as my muscles gripped her hand with each forceful thrust.

"Harder."

She smiled. I could tell she was loving this. I adored that smile. "You're so beautiful when you beg," she said.

Never in my life had I felt anything like this. It was like being stretched—very full, very taken. I wanted to surrender to Gerri so bad, and getting my wish was a dream come true. The more she fucked me the wetter and closer to climaxing I got. The sensation was incredible.

She sucked on my neck while she continued fucking me with her fist. When I didn't think I could take one more excruciating but delicious second, wanting to come so bad it hurt, she placed her mouth on my clit, sucking and licking until my body gave way to the sweet release it longed for. I grasped her baby-fine blonde hair while I came. I thought I heard her gasp when I nearly ripped her hair out of her scalp, so I eased up on the tension and let her silky tresses slip from my fingers. I felt my strength drain from my body in orgasmic bliss.

Gerri rewarded me by releasing her fist slowly from my sated center and gingerly licking my clit some more. Her tongue barely touched me at first while I recovered from the first orgasm, but her ministrations were just enough to get the blood to pool in my clit once more. Expertly she worked my clit and the surrounding swollen areas until I felt the explosion begin again. If I were rating orgasms on a scale from one to ten, this one was a twenty-five. The climax felt like it lasted for hours. I lost all track of time and place until she collapsed on top of me and I kissed her sweaty brow.

"You can fish with me anytime," Gerri said.

"How about tomorrow?"

"Tomorrow is perfect." She flashed me another one of her incredible smiles.

"But next time it's my turn to cast the line," I told her.

"Deal."

I managed to get dressed with a big-ass grin on my face as I looked forward to future fisting—er, I mean fishing.

LONDON, 1988

Maggie Kinsella

Lesbians aren't necessarily the best nurses, but in my opinion nurses are the best lesbians!

In my early twenties, I was working at a busy London hospital and living in the nurses' home. There were about twenty nurses in our residential block, and whether it was a random circumstance, or the manager wanted to keep us happy, about three quarters of us were lesbians. It wasn't one long orgy so much as a small, cozy dating pool. We circulated through each other's rooms like one long game of spin the bottle, kissing, fighting, and making up with equal intensity.

Like many of the other nurses, I made the rounds, seldom staying with the same woman for long. But when I met Marie, things changed. Marie was older than I, in her early thirties, a curvy woman, with a smart wisecracking attitude and a bold manner. She came from Trinidad but had done her nursing training in London as a teenager and had been here ever since.

She had the coveted corner room in the nurses' home, a large room with two windows instead of one.

Marie and I got together one night after we'd both been working the late shift in the operating theater. We were both operating-theater nurses, but she was a senior nurse in urology and normally worked in the older theater block on the other side of the hospital. I had just obtained my first staff-nurse position in the main theater complex.

That night, Marie had been called over to the general surgery area to assist with some emergencies. She and I had the final cleanup, and we were both hurrying. Me, because I was meeting some friends in a nearby pub afterward, and her, I later learned, because she was hoping to waylay another nurse on her way home after her shift.

We chatted as we cleaned to make the time go faster, both of us flirting in an automatic, casual way. She was teasing me about breaking up with Orla, the other Irish nurse in our block. I was retaliating that—knowing Marie's reputation for loving women and moving on—Orla had wanted to settle down with me and raise fine Irish lesbian babies. We were sorting the un-used sutures, and our hands flew over the pile in time with our banter. Our hands both reached for the final catgut suture and our fingertips brushed each other.

I remember that first moment of connection, that first fine thrill that tingled along my fingers. My movement stopped, and my breath caught in my throat. Marie's fingers stilled too.

"Well, well, well," she said, softly. "Fancy that." And then she picked up the suture, put it in the correct box, and moved over to the door of the anaesthetic room. "That bloody technician's left the place a mess again." Her voice sounded amazingly normal.

I struggled to make mine as steady. "I think she got called to ICU," I offered. "She'll be back."

Marie moved into the anaesthetic room and started placing equipment in the sink. I followed her lead and cleared the bench, dumping the glass ampoules and used syringes into the sharps container. I stole a sideways glance at Marie—at her straight back and ripe, round buttocks. She had a wide-legged stance, sturdy legs bracing her full hips. I saw the outline of her thighs through the white dress she wore, and the tantalizing gap between them. Her dress pulled tight over her buttocks, and I saw her panty line.

"So who are you with now that you've escaped Orla's clutches?" she asked.

"No one. My life is barren of a hot woman right now," I sighed in a theatrical manner, and hoped she'd take the hint.

She snorted. "You won't get my sympathy that way."

"Oh? What will it take then?"

She turned from the sink and studied me. "You want a sympathy fuck?"

Now *this* was better! "Not a *sympathy* fuck, no."

The instruments in the sink claimed her attention again, but not before I saw her sudden grin.

"I heard you were easy. Quite the slut."

I pretended affront. "Look who's talking. Remember I've slept with Kate, who slept with Tash, who slept with Bibi—*your* ex-girlfriend. News travels."

"In both directions." She finally gave up all pretence of washing instruments, and turned again, this time to study me blatantly. "Fancy a drink when we finally get out of here?"

I didn't hesitate. "As long as we don't go to the Pig and Tater. I was supposed to meet friends there."

We finished our shift, changed back into street clothes, and without actually discussing it, walked the mile to the Black Horse, a pub that attracted few people from the hospital. I slid into a snug at the back while Marie brought pints over from the bar.

The pub was busy enough that there was a steady hum of conversation, which for me was a good thing. Suddenly I couldn't think of a thing to say.

Marie regarded me with an amused expression. "Oh, fuck this," she said suddenly as the rings reached halfway down my pint. She moved around the snug to sit next to me. Her solid thighs pushed against mine. One of her hands grasped her pint; the other reached down and rested on my own thigh, where her fingers made circular forays around its inner surface. Lightly they tickled, moving slowly in ever-widening spirals, down to my knee and up along my inner thigh.

She started talking: a long rambling story about a friend of hers who was mugged on holiday in Dublin. The words floated over me as I concentrated on those fingers, long skillful fingers, tracing patterns on my jeans.

I stayed silent, willing her to continue, hoping her fingers would drift higher. When her thumb brushed the seam of my jeans, over my cunt, I let out an involuntary gasp. She didn't let up with her story, but I heard the smile in her voice as she continued her tale while her thumb moved slowly to and fro.

I widened my legs slightly and her gentle frottage continued. My jeans were loose enough that she was able to move the seam back and forth and make the thick material press the side of my clit. Each press left and the ripples grew, each press right and my orgasm swelled. My hand clenched on my drink, and I focused on breathing slowly and evenly. I was going to come, and I didn't want the whole pub to hear me screaming, see my head jerking from side to side as my face flushed as dark as the blackcurrant cordial in Marie's pint of lager.

Just as my breath was hitching and I was gulping air, just

before the final big swell when the world would turn crimson, Marie stopped. She withdrew her thumb, moved farther away on the bench, and took a deep draught of her pint. My heart thundered, and I wanted nothing more than for her to continue. I wanted to beg her to push me over the edge, and if I screamed, well, so what? I was beyond being careful. When she didn't move back to finish me off, I dropped my own hand between my thighs.

Her hand snaked out, and grasping my wrist she forced it back to the table. "No," she said, in a voice of steel, one that had made many a junior houseman quail. "Not until I say you can." Her hand moved and clasped mine. "Now it's your round, I believe."

Her grin told me she knew exactly what she was doing. I took a few deep breaths, trying to slide back down from the edge of orgasm. I was afraid to move, afraid that if I walked to the bar, the friction of my jeans between my legs and vibration of my footfalls would be enough to set me off. When the urgency had eased, I stood up and headed for the bar. I thought about going into the ladies' room to bring myself off with my fingers, but the promise in Marie's eyes made me think again. I'd wait.

But I needed to pee, so I did go into the toilet. Dipping a finger into my cunt, I made sure it was fragrant and wet.

I collected the drinks from the bar. When I returned, I ran a casual finger around the rim of Marie's glass.

She noticed immediately, and her eyebrow lifted. "Trying to entice me, Maggie?"

"You don't slide off the hook that easily."

"Oh, you don't need to worry about that." Deliberately she set her lips to the rim and took a long sip. "Delicious!"

After that, our conversation flowed easier. By the time closing time rolled around, I was more than ready to leave. It was a

mild night, and we linked arms and started back to the nurses'
home. London traffic rolled by, at one point coming perilously
close to skimming my hip. As we neared the hospital, Marie
pulled me off to one side, down one of the alleys that led into the
back of the hospital. Away from the lights, and enclosed in the
narrow lane, it was suddenly much darker, much quieter.

We didn't say a word, but our walk became an amble, and
then our feet slowed and stopped. Her arm, which had been
linked through mine, withdrew before wrapping around my
waist. Our faces moved together, and then we were kissing.
Long, slow kisses, wet and passionate, grew more intense as
our passion rose. Her tongue slipped slowly in and out of my
mouth, mine dueled with hers, and our hands made slow forays
over each other.

My hands reached her buttocks, those same ripe buttocks
that had tempted me all evening, and I cupped them, grinding
her into my thigh. She seemed as eager as I, and our movements
grew increasingly frantic. Marie's hands fumbled and grasped
my wrists. She pulled my hands away from her body and pinned
them over my head. She pushed me against the wall, her solid
body trapping me. In the dim light her eyes glittered, and her
voice held a stern air of command.

"Now, you do as you're told!" she said. "You junior nurses
think you know it all. Time you took some lessons from your
seniors."

Exactly what "lessons" she intended teaching was very clear.

She captured my lips once more, kissing me deeply and forcing my head back sharply so that it hit the brick behind me. Her
thigh forced my legs apart, and her hips ground rhythmically
into mine. For a moment I struggled against her restraining
hold. Not because I wanted to break free, but for the excitement
of feeling her strong hands effortlessly holding me in place. I

thought of those same hands holding me down on a bed later.

"Now," she said when she came up for air, "I'm going to let you go. But if you don't bring me off with your tongue in the next few minutes, you'll regret it."

I mentally gulped. *Here?* I thought. *She really means here?*

After freeing my hands, Marie moved to the waist of her jeans. She undid the snaps, then she pushed down her pants. I caught a glimpse of black cotton bikini panties barely visible against her bitter-chocolate skin, and then they were gone, pushed down with her jeans. I forgot about her panties as I saw her dark wiry bush, tight curls hiding the plump cunt mound. She pushed her jeans to her knees and spread her legs as best she could.

My fingers itched to slide into her wetness, but she'd said "tongue." I dropped to my knees on the tarmac, and ignoring the hard surface, I slid my hands up her thighs. Her scent reached me: hot, female, and very, very aroused. My thumbs brushed her pussy lips and she jerked.

"I said tongue," she growled, and she reached down and pulled my hands above my head again. Jerking hard, I toppled against her, my nose in that beautiful black bush. Nuzzling my way down, I parted her lips with my tongue, seeking out her clit. She was slippery-shiny and wet, and her moisture coated my cheeks and chin. I ate her as best I could in my position. My neck and shoulders ached, and her grasp on my wrists increased to near pain. But her taste was intoxicating, as were her own murmurs of satisfaction as her orgasm approached.

Just when I thought my neck would break from the strain, I heard footsteps down the laneway. I tried to rise, move away, but Marie held me effortlessly in place.

"Don't stop!" she whispered.

From the movements of her hips, I sensed she was close to

coming. The footsteps came closer. And then—thank God—
Marie came, pushing her cunt into my face. Her orgasm rushed
hot and salty over my tongue. As her shivers died away, she
released my wrists and pulled me to my feet, wrapping her arms
around my waist. We kissed hungrily again, my body shielding
her disarrayed clothing from view as the unknown footsteps
went past.

She put her clothing to rights, and we continued on, into
the hospital grounds and up to the nurses' home. By unspoken
agreement, we went to her room. It was the first time I'd been
there, and I saw she had put the bed in the corner, underneath
both sets of windows. Her room was on the fifth floor, so it was
high enough to see out over the nearby lights.

Marie went to a cupboard in the corner and poured us
each a glass of ruby port. Drawing me over to her bed, she sat
against the wall, cradling me in her spread thighs, my back to
her breasts. I sipped the sweet liquid and shivered as her hands
came up to caress my breasts. In contrast to her earlier force-
fulness, she was gentle, and she opened my jacket and rubbed
light, teasing circles around my nipples. I arched into her caressing hands, enjoying the sensation and soft stimuli. When she
unbuttoned my shirt and pushed up my bra, her hands on my
bare breasts felt amazing. Nurses' hands are often rough from
vigorous washing, but hers were supple. I looked down at the
erotic contrast of her dark hands against my white skin. I have
large breasts—too large, I often think—but in her hands I felt
they were just right.

When Marie turned me in her arms and kissed me again, I
was putty. She slipped off my clothing, unzipping my jeans and
impatiently pushing them down. Swiftly she removed her clothing, throwing it haphazardly on the floor. Naked, she drew me
down to lie on the bed. The city lights of London washed over

us through the uncurtained windows, painting our skin with a kaleidoscope of reds, golds, and yellows.

Time moved slowly. We'd had the teasing, had the power play. Now, strangely, our loving moved along the scale to tenderness. Marie kissed my breasts, her dark head moving from one to the other. I ran my hands along the curve of her waist, out to her flaring hips, before dipping between. She opened her legs, and my finger insinuated its way into her hot, clasping cunt. For a few minutes, we stayed like that—me with my fingers moving slowly in her cream, her with my nipple between her lips.

Then Marie took charge once more, settling me firmly on my back and coaxing my legs apart. She crouched between them, her face dropping between my thighs, and finally I felt her tongue slide between my pussy lips. I was so horny from before—from the pub, from the laneway, from her hands and mouth on my breasts—that it only took a few flicks of her tongue before I came explosively.

Then, as my cunt relaxed, I felt her fingers probing. Three, maybe four fingers slid inside me, stretching me open, filling me with that delicious weighty fullness, a beautiful ache. Her thumb rubbed slowly to and fro on my nub, and the rolling waves built again to a shivering crescendo.

I stayed with her that night, and for many nights thereafter. Marie was an adventurous lover, and the thrill of potential discovery was one she enjoyed. Often she'd make me eat her in front of her wide windows. It was unlikely that anyone could really see what we were doing up there on the fifth floor, but the potential that maybe, just maybe, someone was watching never failed to bring her to a loud climax. Sometimes she'd make me bend over in front of the window while she fucked me with a strap-on. But other times we'd just spend long hours on her bed, exploring each other with slow mouths and hands.

We dated for nearly six months—a record for Marie—and then I got a position in the local hospital in my hometown in Ireland. It was hard leaving Marie, but I was pleased to be going home. We made the usual promises to stay in touch, but inevitably after a few letters and phone calls, we lost touch.

I still hear about her occasionally, through a friend of a friend, and she's done well for herself. She now heads up the surgical unit in a prestigious teaching hospital in Scotland. Sometimes I daydream of going over and walking into her hospital, trapping her in her office, and eating her out in front of a bunch of wide-eyed junior doctors.

I think the exhibitionist in her would enjoy that!

SCARS

Nell Stark

She kisses my scars when we make love.

The smallest is a thin line just above my left eyebrow, from a high school basketball game. One of the opposing players swung an elbow into my face as I went up for a shot at the bottom of the key. The pain was sharp, but I didn't realize that the skin had split until I reached up to brush the sweat off my forehead and my hand came away red.

Head injuries bleed hard. Makes sense, I guess—there's a lot going on under there. Thousands of tiny pathways crisscrossing back and forth, over and under, like a cloverleaf on the interstate. All of them throbbing in time, in harmony...and in the next second, broken and gushing. But I don't even remember the pain as clearly as the surprise: the sudden knowledge that, really, anything can cut. At the right time, in the right place, even a misplaced elbow can take four stitches.

The swelling faded after a few weeks, but the scar is still there if you know where to look. And she does. Her lips trace it a few times, drawing out the memory of rupture then soothing it back to sleep under my skin. I close my eyes and exhale slowly, feeling my body conform to the contours of the bed. Her mouth is soft and will not break me.

She kisses down the length of my nose and pauses at the left corner of my mouth. My fist clenches as her tongue flicks lightly across my lips. They part for her—but she is moving on, across my cheek to suckle on my earlobe before trailing her mouth down the side of my neck. I tilt my head to make it easier for her, and she hums against my collarbone.

Her teeth gently nip at the skin where my neck intersects my shoulder, and my body shifts restlessly against the soft blanket. The touch of her mouth is a thread of fire radiating out from the soft licks of her tongue. Sewing me together—across my shoulder, swirling over the light bulge of my biceps, tasting the indentation of my elbow.

When she pauses there, I can't help whimpering. It's so very sensitive. My toes flex—down and back—in time to the movements of her lips. I'm about to beg her to touch me, but she finally moves on, raising my arm so she can run her tongue along the strip of thick, pale skin just beyond the joint.

I fell off my bike, that day. I was eight years old and gangly, lacking the grace to save myself. Hit the asphalt hard with my hands, and they burned. I remember turning them over, seeing the tiny pieces of asphalt embedded in my palms like flecks in marble. Didn't even feel the gash on my arm, until my mother's shrill exclamation. Even then, it was only a dull, persistent throbbing, matching the low roar of the car's engine on the way to the ER.

When I begged them not to give me stitches, they didn't—even though they should have. Instead a young male resident dug the grit out of my hands, stuck a glorified Band-Aid on my forearm, and sent me home. Later that night I screamed as my parents poured hydrogen peroxide over the gaping mouth of the cut. Hydrogen peroxide, the refiner's fire. It frothed and bubbled, like madness. Keep it clean, keep it pure. Free of contagion.

That worked, for a while.

The fingers of her right hand trail along my left side, tracing the bumps of my rib cage before sliding into the dip between my leg and abdomen. She is so close to *really* touching me, this way, and the low whimper that escapes from my mouth is involuntary. But after a tantalizing moment, she continues on, ever so slowly, until she finds the slash of rippled skin on the front of my knee. Her mouth continues to caress my arm, connecting the dots—elbow to knee, scar to scar, pleasure to pleasure. Her fingers also burn, but it's different. I don't scream, though I might later.

I fell again, in high school, on a ski slope. This, also, was a test of grace. Took a wrong turn and landed in a mogul field—huge, steep bumps with nothing but ice in between—and somersaulted over the crest of one to land in the chill trough. I felt, more than heard, the pop in my knee. Tried to stand and fell again.

ACL. This time, my body rebelled against itself—bone tearing through the ligament, severing it in two. My first thought, lying there while I waited for the ski patrol, was that I wouldn't be able to finish the basketball season. That I'd disappoint Melinda—the captain, my hero. Senior to my freshman. She'd be sad for me, and worried, but also angry. If only I hadn't made that turn, if I'd been better. If only I'd gone more slowly.

The whole trip down the mountain, strapped to a stretcher behind the bright red snowmobile, I saw her disappointed expression on the insides of my eyelids. The tears leaked out to freeze on my face.

Three months later I had the surgery. By that time the muscles had grown strong again. I was walking—mostly without a limp—only to be returned to crutches in the wake of the operation. Back to basics, one more time—to infancy, to helplessness. A seething stasis. The doctor cut out a piece of my patella tendon, made it into a new ligament, and screwed it into my traitorous bones. Good as new, he said.

But it isn't, not quite. It still twinges, from time to time, in memory of the knife. Some wounds never heal, and this is mine.

She pays special attention to it, caressing it with slow, gentle touches—the way she'll stroke me elsewhere, soon enough. My breaths are gasps, my hips in motion. Then her fingers move slowly *up*, swirling around the slight bulge of my quads before trailing farther along my thigh, up and up and up. A low groan escapes my lips as she traces the contours of my hip bone.

Her lips meet her fingers a few inches above and to the right of my navel. At the top of my first scar. She rests her chin on my belly for a moment, so that she can meet my eyes.

"I love you," she says. Her voice is soft and deep and gritty with desire. Sandpaper, to smooth out my jagged edges.

"Love you back," I whisper. The surge of my pelvis is involuntary. She grins and returns her mouth to the top of the long, thin line.

Ileal atresia. Simply put, the absence of an opening in part of the small intestine. Almost half of mine was solid. I couldn't keep any food down, of course—vomited it up almost immediately. It wouldn't have taken long for my premature body to poison itself. So there I was, a day and a half old and five weeks early, taking up a fraction of the operating table as the surgeon cut into my abdomen, removed the malformed tissue, and reconnected the ends. I spent a few weeks in an incubator after that. No one could touch me without wearing gloves for the first month of my life. Is it any wonder, then, that I'm starving for her hands on me, every chance I get?

I came out wrong. Defective. Incomplete. Flawed. God could have recalled me but didn't. On the bad days, I think He should have. Sometimes I think my parents wish they could cut this part of me out too: the part that needs her mouth, her hands, her love. Cut her out of me and reconnect the pieces, make me a straight girl after all.

But if I hadn't come out wrong, would I truly appreciate this? Breathing, running, feeling, *being*? And her, would I appreciate her? Would I know what I have, if that long, thin line weren't there to remind me every morning in the mirror?

Her fingers leave the base of the scar to trail through the curly patch of hair farther south. My breaths are short and sharp as she finds my wetness, as she draws the moisture up and over my swollen clitoris. Gradually, her lips follow the same path, until the warm puffs of her breaths cascade over me in counterpoint to the teasing motions of her hand.

As she takes me into her mouth and enters me tenderly with one long finger, I forget that I am broken. On the good days, I know I was made exactly as I was meant to be. On the good days, she unifies my body with her fingers, lips, words.

On the good days, I am whole.

BY ANY OTHER NAME

Kristina Wright

There are times when living with someone can be a joy. Waking to a warm body beside you, her scent on your pillow. Having a friendly face to hold your hand across the dinner table as you recount the adventures of the day. Sharing your toaster and your heart with someone who knows you better than you know yourself. Yeah, living with someone can be wonderful.

And then there are the days where you'd give anything to live alone, with no one to worry about except yourself and maybe a goldfish. As I stared at the red Honda parked in front of my townhouse, I contemplated the perks of fish ownership.

Rosalie was home.

I coasted my bike to a stop, reluctant to go inside. She had stormed out the night before, angry and silent, leaving me to guess what the hell I'd done wrong.

I'd been up most of the night alternating between worrying about her and being mad because she *knew* I was worrying

about her. I called her office in the morning, but the bitchy re-
ceptionist said she was out showing houses all day. By six, I'd
worked myself into a self-righteous frenzy. Rosalie could be a
moody wench when she wanted to be, and I was in no mood to
put up with it.

I was half-tempted to turn my bike around and spend
the night at the library. Let her worry for a change. Instead
I grabbed my books out of the handlebar basket and headed
toward the house. Rosalie always said I looked like a schoolgirl with my long red braids and shiny yellow bike. I told her I
was still a schoolgirl—a twenty-six-year-old perpetual student.
I was finishing my degree in Women's Studies at Florida State
and working at the library in the evenings. When Rosalie had a
couple of glasses of wine in her, she would leer and say she could
teach me all I needed to know about women. She was right.

I opened the front door and breathed in her unique scent of
organic lavender shampoo and baby powder. No matter how
mad I was, the smell of her made my heart flip-flop in my chest.
I heard the shower shut off. My first impulse was to confront her
and ask her where the hell she'd been. I decided that was exactly
what she expected me to do. So instead I grabbed a bottle of
juice out of the fridge and curled up in a chair with a biography
of Margaret Mead. Let Rosalie come to me for a change.

She walked into the room buck naked, a white towel wrapped
around her head turban-style. "I didn't hear you come in."

I have to say, Rosalie looks better naked than most women
do clothed. I tried to ignore the way her breasts swayed as she
leaned over to grab an apple from the bowl on the table next to
me. Her nipples were tightly puckered and as rosy as her name.
I looked her over, hungry for her body but still angry at her for
walking out.

"I didn't think you cared," I said. Despite my best intentions,

I couldn't help noticing she'd trimmed her thick, dark muff into a neat little triangle.

"What the hell is that supposed to mean?" She looked like Eve tempting me with her apple.

I turned back to my book. "You're the one who took off. You didn't even bother calling." I sounded like a petulant child, but damn, she'd hurt me. She'd never been gone all night before.

"I was angry," she said softly. She tossed the apple back in the bowl. "You made me feel like shit last night."

Last night I'd dragged Rosalie to my family reunion despite her protests. We'd been together for nearly a year, and I thought it was about time to inflict my family on her. Everybody knew I was partial to girls, and Mom had long since given up on finding the right boy for me, thank God. It was funny to watch soft-spoken Rosalie in the midst of my boisterous clan.

"What did I do?" I asked, genuinely baffled.

I thought the evening had gone quite well. Even Gran had been smitten with Rosalie, and that woman doesn't like anyone who isn't Irish, or at least Catholic. Rosalie had been quieter than usual, but I chalked it up to nerves. It wasn't until we got home that I realized she was giving me the silent treatment. When I finally asked what her problem was, she split.

"There were thirty people there and you never once introduced me as anything other than your friend."

I closed my book and put it aside, trying to avoid the accusation in her eyes. I'd had two relationships go really bad. She knew that. I thought it was a pretty big step just bringing her to my parents' house. One look into those stormy dark eyes told me differently.

"So? What do you want me to call you?" I asked, torn between frustration and anger. Rosalie was always pushing for more than I wanted to give.

She strode across the room and stood in front of me, fisting her hands on her hips. Water droplets clung to her heavy breasts and the soft curve of her stomach. "Hell, I don't care. Anything would be better than, 'This is my friend, Rosalie.'"

I didn't like her tone. I stood up and brushed past her. "You're being ridiculous."

"Wait a minute. We're not finished here." She grabbed my arm and pushed me back in the chair. I couldn't do anything but gape at her. Rosalie is as sweet and gentle as they come. She can be a hellion in bed, but we weren't in bed and I was starting to get pissed off.

"Knock it off, Rose," I said, not at all liking the nasty little smirk she gave me. "I need a shower."

She knelt in front of me and spread my thighs with her hands. "What you need is to learn some manners."

Before I could speak, she slid her hand up my skirt and cupped my crotch. A wave of heat spread through my belly and I groaned. She had that effect on me. One touch and I was lost. Instantly, I spread my legs wider to allow her access, all thoughts of anger fleeing my mind as moisture flooded my crotch.

"You're hot." She toyed with the elastic on my underwear. "Are you wet?"

I knew my cunt was already slick with my juices. "Why don't you find out?" I gasped when her finger burrowed under the leg of my panties.

"Yeah, wet." She finger-fucked me gently, her baby-soft finger gliding inside me. "I love how wet you get."

The material of my panties restricted her motions, but her finger felt good inside my fevered cunt. My clit throbbed against the thin fabric of my panties, aching to be touched. I leaned my head against the chair and closed my eyes. Suddenly the finger was gone and I felt empty.

"Don't stop," I said, hearing a hint of desperation in my voice. Then it dawned on me that was what she wanted. "Touch me, Rose."

She sat back on her knees, one delicate eyebrow arched. She looked like some exotic harem girl in her towel turban, kneeling before me in supplication. But we both knew who was in charge. "Touch me, what?"

"Please?"

She laughed, but I could tell by the hitch in her voice that she was getting turned on too. "No, you said, 'Touch me, Rose.' What else could you call me?"

I grinned at her little game. Did I mention she can be a devious wench? "Touch me, baby."

She nodded, the towel on her head wobbling. "Better."

She pushed my panties to the side and pushed her finger inside me again. I arched my hips off the chair and felt her go deeper. When I started rocking on her finger, she pulled it away again. I sighed in frustration.

"Take off your skirt," she said. "Just your skirt."

I eagerly complied, stripping off my skirt and spreading my legs once more. The crotch of my panties was already soaked through and clinging to the plump lips of my cunt. Rosalie leaned forward and inhaled my scent, not quite touching me.

"Mmm, you smell good," she said. "What do you want?"

"Touch me," I pleaded.

"Touch me..." she prompted.

I reached down and tugged the towel from her head, letting her long, damp hair cascade over my thighs. "Touch me, sweetheart."

She nuzzled me with her lips, nipping my clit through the wet cotton. I groaned and tangled my hands in her hair but she pushed them away and put them over my breasts. I pinched my hard nipples through my T-shirt, aching to feel her mouth on them. When I raised my crotch closer to her face, she moved away.

"Are you ashamed of me?" She said it with a smile, but I saw the vulnerability in her expression.

I wrapped my arms and legs around her and pulled her close. "Of course not, baby. I love you."

"So the next time I meet your family, you'll introduce me properly?" She pulled away and teased my clit through the fabric once more.

I nodded, wanting her. Needing her. "I promise."

"Lift up." I raised my ass so she could tug my panties off. She slid them down my legs and tossed them over her shoulder. They landed on a lamp like a jaunty pink beret. "How will you introduce me?"

"I'll think of something," I said. "Now stop teasing me. Please."

She blew air over my engorged cunt and I gasped. "What will you say?"

"Whatever you want."

Rosalie had the nerve to shake her finger at me. The same finger she'd been fucking me with. "No. You tell me. I want to hear it."

"Touch me, Rose," I begged. "Lick me."

"Introduce me."

"Fine." I groaned in agony. My cunt was on fire and she wanted to play mind games. "This is my girlfriend, Rosalie."

A frown crinkled her brow. "Hmm. Better. Is that the best you can do?"

I was spread wide in front of her, her mouth inches from my swollen clit. My juices dripped from my cunt and down my crack, tickling my ass. I was probably leaving a wet spot on the chair. I didn't give a damn. "My significant other."

Her fingertip found my opening. "Too cold. I'm tired of your feminist bullshit. What else?"

I squirmed and clenched my muscles, trying to suck her finger into me. I groaned when I felt her go a little deeper. "My roommate."

The finger retreated. "That's worse than friend."

I moaned, my brain searching frantically for something that would please her. "My lover."

Rosalie cooed and the finger slid all the way inside. "That's nice. Very brave." Her thumb made gentle circles around my asshole and I whimpered.

She fucked me like that for a bit, her finger bumping my cervix as she massaged the walls of my cunt. I pushed my hips up to meet her thrusts and her thumb lodged against my asshole. After a while one finger wasn't enough, I was too wet. I wanted to feel more of her.

"Please, baby," I said. "Give me more."

She withdrew her finger and hooked her hands under my thighs, pushing my legs up on the arms of the chair. I was spread as wide as I could go, the lips of my cunt stretched taut, exposing me to her gaze. She bent her head and I felt her breath. So close. So damn close.

"C'mon, Rose, don't tease me." I mauled my tits in frustration, wanting her to touch me and yet secretly thrilled by her newfound dominance.

"I like *lover*," she said, sounding as prim and proper as any librarian I'd ever worked with. "But it's a little blunt. What else do you have?"

I shook my head. I couldn't think.

"Tell me." Her fingernail lightly scraped the side of my clit and I jumped. "Tell me and I'll suck you until you come."

Every muscle in my body quivered with need. I stared into

her flushed face, seeing passion and something more. Something so tender and honest, it brought tears to my eyes.

"My love," I whispered. "This is Rosalie, my love."

I was rewarded by her brilliant smile. I had only a moment to enjoy it before she tucked her hands under my ass and raised my soaked crotch to her mouth. I groaned and squirmed against her face as she plunged her tongue into me. She feasted on my cunt lips and then moved up to my swollen clit, sucking it between her lips. She slid one hand up my thigh and used two fingers to fuck me hard and fast. I could hear the wet, squishy sounds of my cunt as I screamed her name over and over.

I came so hard I got an instant, blinding headache. She gently nursed on my quivering clit as I floated back to earth. The pain in my head faded to a dull ache as I looked down at her. Her mouth glistened with my juices while her fingers still made lazy circles inside me. I squeezed those fingers and smiled wickedly.

"What?" she asked, licking her lips.

I pulled her up on my lap and kissed her, loving the taste of me on her mouth. Gathering her damp hair in my hand, I tilted her head back to look at her. "What would you have done if I'd called you the old ball-and-chain?"

She reached down and tweaked my still-sensitive clit with her thumb and forefinger. "Why don't you find out?"

I grinned and squirmed before pushing her off my lap and leading her toward the bedroom. I decided I didn't really want a goldfish after all.

BRONCO BUTCHES

Ellen Tevault

I know, the sexual confessions of a femme who loves a butch with a strap-on—or do I mean a strap-on with a butch?—is a given. Well, this tomboyish femme's sexual desires have landed her in some trouble.

Once I brought up the topic of butches and strap-ons in a butch-femme e-group, and for my views on the topic, I received a staunch thrashing from the other femmes. Of course, the butches remained silent.

The first time I tried it was more than ten years ago with a past girlfriend, Gina. Up until then, I hadn't used a strap-on, but one day it happened.

As we cuddled in bed, I said, "I bought a strap-on today." I avoided Gina's gaze and waited for her reaction. Since we'd only been dating a week, I didn't know what to expect.

"Let me see it." When I heard a lilt in her voice, I glanced at her face and saw a beaming smile.

"Really?" I stared at her, not knowing what to do. "Have you ever used one?"

"No, but I've always wanted to." Gina pulled me close and held me. "A lot of femmes love them."

"Yeah." I sighed, not knowing how to ask what I wanted to at that moment.

"Now, go get it." She gently pushed me away. "Please. Let's try it."

After a few long seconds I crawled out of bed and snatched the bag from the closet. I handed it to Gina and watched her open it as I played nervously with my hair.

She pulled the cock and strap from the bag with a wicked grin. When she saw the contraption, she furrowed her brow.

"It's a cheap one," I told her. I crawled back into bed and looked over her shoulder at it. "Will it work?"

"We'll make it work." She threaded the elastic strap around her thick waist. "Boy, where'd you get this?" She snapped the elastic strap onto the cock base.

"Susan and I went to that store on Pendleton Pike." I grinned, thinking about how our friend Terry had refused to go with us. "You know, the one with the peep shows in the back room."

Gina chuckled. "Yeah, I wouldn't be caught dead in there. Too scary." She pulled me close, and I felt the cock bounce against my thigh. "You went in there? You are one tough femme to do that, darling."

"Yeah?" I giggled. "I wanted one."

"Well, when we can afford it, we'll buy a better one. One with a leather harness." As she talked, she slid the cock between my lips. "We'll do our best with this one, though." She thrust her hips, and I felt the cock fill me up.

"Hmm, that feels good." I wrapped my legs around Gina's

husky frame as she slid the cock in and out. "Oh, yeah, deeper."

She responded by slapping her body against my thighs. As the cock penetrated my deepest recesses, I shuddered and screamed.

"Give it to me, baby," she grunted as she held my thighs and slammed into me. "Don't hold it back. Come for me."

I groaned as my orgasm shot from me and I collapsed onto the bed. Gina brushed my hair out of my face and kissed me. I shivered and shuddered more as she held me.

"Feel good?" She kissed my head.

"Good," I whispered into her chest.

After a few minutes of recuperating and cuddling, I asked the unthinkable. "Have you ever received?"

"Received what?" She brushed her fingers through my hair.

I paused and licked my lips as I thought about how to ask for what I wanted. "Received?" I pointed to the cock as I spoke.

Gina's hand froze in my hair, when she realized what I meant. My breathing quickened as I waited for her to respond.

"Have you done this before?" she asked.

"Done what?" I wanted to look up at her, but I couldn't.

"You, you know," she said, lacing her fingers through my long, dark hair.

"No, I've never been on either end of one until tonight."

"Really?" Gina chuckled. "I would've never known."

"Oh, shut up." I play-slugged her and giggled. I didn't know if she was trying to change the subject, so I resigned myself to letting it drop.

She sighed and whispered her response so softly I almost didn't hear it. "Okay."

I jerked my head up and looked at her. "What?"

"You heard me." She unsnapped the cock and handed it to me. "Do you need help putting it on?"

"I don't know." Suddenly I felt overwhelmed and wondered if I should do it.

"Let me help." Gina wrapped the elastic around my waist and snapped the cock into place. I watched her secure it. When she finished, she smiled at me. "It's okay. You'll be fine."

"Are you sure?" I raised one eyebrow as I spoke.

"I wouldn't have said yes if I wasn't." She nuzzled my neck, which electrified my spine.

"Have you ever?" I gulped and motioned to the cock.

"No." She shook her head. "You'd be my first, too."

"Really?" I bit my lip and smiled. "Really?" I laughed. "Goodie."

Gina leaned back and pulled me on top of her. "Are you ready, baby?"

"Yeah, I am." I kissed her before I leaned up and gripped her ample thighs. "Oh, God," I said. A power rush like none I'd felt before overcame me as I slid the cock into my big, luscious butch and she sighed with ecstasy. I watched her face as I worked the toy in and out. She closed her eyes and bit her lip between sighs.

At first it felt awkward trying to guide the cock with my hips. I wanted to feel it like guys do, but I could only imagine the heat of her cunt seeping into its flesh. Every so often I flicked my eyes away from her face to watch the cock enter her again. I licked my lips as I saw it open her lips and penetrate her.

"Oh, God." My body and time moved in slow motion with every sensation on high. "Does that feel good?"

"Better than I thought," she said, bucking against me as I pushed forward.

With her guidance I grabbed on to her thighs and sped up my movements to match her needs. When I thought my hips would give out on me, she clenched her jaw, grunted, and shuddered in orgasm.

I collapsed on top of her, and she held me to her chest. I felt her breathing slow from a pant to a steady release. She brushed my hair away from my face and kissed my forehead. When I looked up at her, I didn't know what to expect. She smiled groggily.

After that moment, I was hooked on the power of giving such pleasure, especially to a butch.

A few years later, I met my hersband, Melissa, who was basically a virgin. She'd never received in bed, except for a little experimenting with men.

"I don't know. It wasn't that great when I was with them," she said, referring to penetration with the men. "I ended up lying there wondering what the hell all the fuss was about. This is it?" She shrugged her arms.

"Please, just once." I lowered my eyes and bit my lip. "Just once. If you don't like it, we won't ever try it again."

After a few long quiet moments, Melissa said, "Just once?" She paused and glanced over to the strap-on. "Okay? Once?"

She helped me fasten the strap around my plump waist and the others around my thighs. "I don't know about that cock. It looks awfully big," she said. She rummaged through the toy box. "Here it is. Mr. Slim Jim." She chuckled. "He's just right." She swapped the cocks on the strap-on and smiled.

"Are you sure you haven't done this before?"

"Yep, I'm sure, so go slow." Melissa leaned back and slid a pillow under her hips. "Be gentle with me. I'm fragile, you know."

"You are such a jokester. How can I take you seriously?" I lunged at her.

She wrestled with me as she said, "Because you can." Once I'd pinned her down, I teased her clit with my free hand. "Hey, that's cheating," she said. She wiggled in such a way that I couldn't tell if she wanted to get away or get closer, so I stayed with her. "Oh, God." She threw her head back and sighed. "Woman, you're incredible. You make me feel things I thought I'd never feel."

"Good." I cuddled against her and kissed her neck's curve. "That's what I want."

"You know, you scare the hell out of me." She chuckled, but I knew she meant it by the tone of her voice.

"It wouldn't be the first time," I said as I rose onto my knees, tilted my head, and shot her my innocent look.

She ruffled my hair. "I bet. You don't fool me."

"I don't?" I mocked disappointment. "Darn it."

Melissa and I both laughed until an uncomfortable silence enveloped us. She stared at me, and I struggled with whether or not I should make the next move. I trailed my hands over her full thighs and enjoyed the soft, warm flesh. I inched my hips into place between her legs, and the cock nudged against her thigh.

"Oh, boy," she sighed as I approached.

"Changing your mind?" I paused for a response. "I'll stop. It's okay."

She shook her head and wrapped her legs around me, which trapped me between her thighs. "I said I would."

I worked my hand between her legs and stroked her lips. Moisture lubed my hand as I manipulated her silky folds.

"Hmm, that feels good." She loosened her grip around my waist. "Oh, yeah."

After I worked her moisture over the cock, I slid it in inch by inch until it was buried inside her hot hole. I paused for her to get used to the penetration. When she bucked against me, I knew it was time to give her what she craved. I worked it in and out at a steady beat as she squirmed and latched onto the head-board and mattress corner with her hands.

"I need more. Deeper."

Hearing those words, an animalistic desire overcame me. I raised her thighs between us, reached over her head for the headboard, and pumped my hips the fastest I'd ever ridden. I felt the headboard squish my fingers against the wall, but I ignored it as she bucked against me. The more she screamed the faster and harder I wanted to give it to her.

"Whose feet?" she panted, looking around. "Oh, who gives a shit? Keep going." She yelled a string of words I didn't under-stand, which I took as encouragement.

Finally, sweat dripped and pooled between us as I rode my butch.

"Come on, baby. Give it to me." I encouraged her through pants and moans.

"Oh, shit." She stretched those two words out for a few sec-onds before she collapsed.

I fell on top of Melissa, breathing heavily.

"Oh, shit." She slowly withdrew her hands from the spots they'd been holding on to. "Oh, shit."

"Is that all you can say?" I lifted my head off her chest and glanced up at her. "You, okay?"

She nodded and licked her lips. We lay there for half an hour or more before she spoke again. "Whose feet were those?"

"What? What are you talking about?"

She lifted her hand slowly and held it within inches of her face. "The feet that were right here. Whose were they?"

I giggled. "I think they were yours." A blush rose to my face as I thought about it.

"Oh, shit, honey." She pulled me to her. "Honey? I don't think big girls are supposed to fold in half like that." She chuckled and kissed the top of my head. "Not that I'm complaining or anything."

Melissa and I cuddled and dozed off and on. During one of our alert moments, I asked, "So is it a one-time thing? Or can we do it again sometime?"

"Definitely again. You ain't getting off that easy." She tickled me. "I'm keeping score of your talents and making a schedule of future demonstrations."

I giggled and tickled her back. "How about being my bad boy sometime?"

She furrowed her eyebrows and said, "What does that mean?" She thought for a minute and smiled. "So is that why you like to watch those anal videos?"

"Yeah." I glanced at her for a reaction, embarrassed she'd figured it out so easily.

"We'll see, darling. Oh, boy will we see." She paused and stared at the ceiling. "Bad boy? Is that what you want to call it?" She nodded. "If you're a good girl, I'll be your bad boy."

NYC

Rowan Elizabeth

I always want to kiss Cleo. Every single time I'm near her. She makes me feel sensual and erotic by her very presence. Cleo sees the world as a poet does, lyrically. She brings me to views I haven't yet seen, elegant words in an often-skewed perspective. She finds divine details to decorate her life. We met in the days of dancing, drink, and unabashed lust. It was a time when I surrounded myself with passionate people.

In those days, my heart belonged to my dearest friend, Liz, and she was irreplaceable. Small, muscular, and dark, she had an exotic quality that drew people to her. Her father was an excommunicated priest, her mother the Bolivian beauty that seduced him from the Lord. I had met Liz on the porch of a house shared by our friends. She swung in the hammock and invited me to work out with her. I said yes just to be near her. It was the beginning of an understanding. We would know all about each other. We do to this day.

Liz and I would often find ourselves in rich restaurants or pounding clubs, yet we never found ourselves in bed together. We loved each other as sisters, with a strange bent, and were extraordinarily protective of each other. We each looked after the other's heart, while at the same time we led each other into delicious destruction whenever we could.

We would take great pains to prepare ourselves for our long nights of carnal delights. In the slope-ceilinged attic apartment of a downtown house, we'd begin drinking wine and occasional tequila that would continue throughout the night, and fussed for perfection. We flung ourselves around to cheap audiocassettes of dance mixes that had been given to us by DJs at our favorite haunts. We finalized with a brazen application of the deepest red lipstick and escaped into what I always remember as cold nights. Close together in Liz's small white car with her inadequate heater.

It was in the dark, smoky club NYC—a deteriorating storefront building with great glass windows and one large room serving as a bar—that we danced like heathens. The decadent were funneled into a much smaller room in the back to dance. Sweat, deafening music; pulsing, throbbing bodies in a claustrophobic's nightmare.

Beautiful gay men and divine women of variable sexualities forced themselves into the small room. On a platform, someone would be dancing in nothing but jockeys or a gladiator harness, sometimes getting fondled by another dancer. I'd enter the room as if pushing through a wall. That moment removed me from the reality I knew and brought me into the dream I kept. I'd shut my eyes and fall into the music. Sometimes alone, usually terrifyingly close to someone else. When all I wanted to do was dance without the constriction of another, Liz and I would create our own space of gruff attitudes to seal ourselves from intrusion. Liz smelled of patchouli, alcohol, cigarettes, and the lingering scents of other women. I'd drop into the rhythm, take in her scent, and simply exist in the bursting lights and fervor of the music.

We danced in the days of techno, deep house, and trance, a tirade of heavy beats fleshed out with electronic creations. DJ Jonathan fed us from his perch high in the corner booth. The music oozed sexual innuendo, rhythmic fucking, and driving ecstasy. There was a base feeling to the sound that implied so much more than dancing.

We'd take drugs and fill ourselves with wine. Liz and I would dance with Dawn, Peggy, and Angelita in the haze. Barb would press Liz against the support beam in the center of the room, while half-naked Angelita attempted to seduce me. Mandy, soft with white skin and clad as a Goth girl, would become emotional at any attention. There were so many of the eclectic tribe. We lived a life of excess: these extraordinary women, Liz, and I. Extraordinary women like Cleo.

I would come to find that Cleo had always been bold. It was through her boldness that I came to know her.

Late on a Saturday night, in the depths of NYC, I was shaken out of my trance by the sudden appearance of the woman. I watched as the tall redhead lost herself to the music. Cleo moved with a piercing energy. Her arms were raised into the cloud of man-made smoke, her swath of red hair swinging to cover her shoulders and eyes. I stared. It had always been one of my bad habits, and most often I didn't care who noticed. When she caught me, though, I felt suddenly weak. All of my personal power, my high self-opinion, drained from me into this woman.

Cleo crossed the small room, passing through the throng of the hypnotized. I can't say whether her full mouth smiled when she reached me or if she just took hold of me. I felt her long fingers move around my waist to the small of my back. We slipped into the music. She was so direct in her gaze, until she shut her eyes, leaning her forehead into mine.

Our hips and breasts came together as Cleo pressed closer. Her body was firm and athletic in contrast to my softer, rounder form. She was taller than me, her shoulders broader than my own. Her hand lay firmly on the curve of my waist. Her scent was rich with expensive perfume and sweat. Our movements became fluid, and my arm wrapped around her shoulders, my hand was in her hair. I pulled it to my face, rubbing it against my cheek and up into my own hair. She must have sprinkled the perfume through her hair. Years later that scent would still stir my senses.

I couldn't tell you how long we danced that way, fused. The music moved through me, through her, and created a concoction of energy. It wrapped around us and pulled us closer. I silently turned away any of my previous dance partners with a brash gaze or a sharp hand to stay with Cleo. In the middle of the morning, the music stopped and the lights came up. Liz came to fetch me, possessively wrapped her arms around my shoulders, and pulled me away. Cleo stepped back, lightly kissed me on the mouth, turned, and left.

I could never imagine wanting to pull away from Liz, until the night I almost chased Cleo.

The following week I went back to NYC and scoured the crowd for any sign of Cleo. I sought friends, acquaintances, anyone who could tell me about the woman. She was married, but no one ever saw her and her husband together. She was an artist, and several people wore the jewelry she made. She came to the club to dance every weekend, was rarely seen anywhere else.

I sat at a small table in the main open room. I watched

through the large, plate-glass store windows, waiting for Cleo to arrive. I wandered to the bathrooms and talked with a queen who thought I had "tremendous breasts." I told her she had beautiful eyes, took my turn, and returned to my table. I saw Liz dancing in the adjacent room. Between mixes, she'd shoot a look of concern in my direction. But she was too busy with—oh, I don't remember the girl's name, although I met her later. Liz would always tell me she knew I was lost. She loved me and knew I was happiest when I was lost.

It was past two in the morning when Cleo arrived. Laughing and open, she moved through the crowd. She belonged in this environment of extravagance. I finished my wine and summoned the lust that would carry my limping courage. NYC wasn't the type of place where you asked to dance with someone—you merely stepped up and began.

I slid in behind Cleo and wrapped my arm around her waist. She turned in my grasp with a sliding fluidity that would give her a moment to decide if she wished to dance with her intruder. She smiled at me in recognition and firmly kissed me on the lips. I braced her head with my hand and prolonged her greeting. Cleo's tongue danced over the edges of my mouth and I took her lower lip into mine for a punctuated suck. "Apotheosis" chanted in the small room. We surrendered to the rocking, jabbing sounds. The kiss had given me confidence, and I rocked my hips into the firm smoothness of Cleo's body. Our energy increased as we came together in the heat and the smoke and the driving rhythm.

We were willing to go as far as the music and the room took us. Willing to dance as pagans under the throbbing lights and become as nocturnal as the music called us to be. I rushed my hand into the long locks of the red hair that had first found my attention and pulled her into a violent kiss. Cleo, not in the slightest disarmed, chewed my lips until I'm sure they should have bled. I spread my fingers and ran them over her collarbone and down to one of her breasts, firm and delicious. I felt Cleo's long fingers unsnap the front of my suede vest, exposing my encased breasts. I took off my lace bra and hooked it through my belt. At NYC a spontaneous undressing was barely noticed.

The hypnotized crowd danced around us in physical concoctions. The deep beat of the music drove me closer to Cleo. Her long fingers manhandled the tops of my breasts. She lowered her head to my exposed nipple. "Injected with a Poison" blared throughout the room. Grasping Cleo's deft mouth to my breast, I groaned into the music, and her vicious, gnawing sucking.

I grabbed her shoulders and forced her from me, back into the concrete block wall behind her. Pressed against her mouth, her body, I forced my hand into the waist of her trim pants. Cleo squirmed to allow me access. My fingers met the willing wetness of Cleo deep within the heat of her snug trousers. I found her proud clit and grasped it between two fingers. She arched into me, digging long fingers into my flesh. We both would be bruised from the assault.

Cleo grabbed my wrist and wrestled it from her pants. I felt an urgent need to touch her again. She pulled me through the delirious crowd toward the bathroom. We escaped behind the purple door, and Cleo locked it tight. Her grip on my wrist was a painful pleasure. Up against the door, we slammed our bodies together. Hands and mouths moved in a frenzy.

Violent kisses coupled with strong hands on pliable flesh. Music rushed through us. We'd found a like rhythm with our desperate hands. The realization that anything could happen in this club, in the middle of this city, struck Cleo and me at the same instant. I dropped to my knees in the swill of the spilled drinks and questionable liquids that covered the bathroom floor, soaking my jeans.

I tore at the button and zipper of her trousers, at the filmy material of her panties. Discretion was lost to the pounding music, the stroking, the possible climax. I pulled Cleo's pants down over her hips and buried my face in the limited exposure. I felt her full lower lips, full with the blood of excitement. I pressed my hand through the folds of her to her core, forcing myself inside with the latest blast of music. I tilted her hips toward me, pulling with my fingers inside her. I stretched my tongue beyond its limits to find the first taste of her, raw and earthy, and I clasped onto her clit.

Cleo planted her hand in my hair, begging, exciting, demanding more. I forced my fingers, two, then three into her, curved toward the ideal spot. Her hips convulsed as I sucked deeply on her clit. I thought I could hear her gasps above the music, her moans over the rhythm, yet I'm sure now the sounds were mine.

Covered in liquor, awash in the music, I knelt in service. Cleo's smooth interior muscles clenched my fingers. I heard her breathing slow, regaining her elegant demeanor. I came up to press the taste of her onto her own lips. Cleo, in her infinite poise, managed to slow my desperate kisses. She ran her hand across my face, forced me to look her in the eye. She petted me to a stop. I twitched with the desire to grab her, to maul her. She stroked my arms, the swell of my breasts. She calmed me as one would a child or an injured animal. And then she kissed me. With such delicacy. I wanted to please her, to prove I was capable of the unlabored dignity she desired. I had to breathe, slowly and with definite purpose. Cleo once again kissed my lips, my cheeks, my eyelids. She pulled her pants around her hips as she soothed me. She then began to talk to me.

Cleo and I have talked ever since. We have kissed every time we have met or left each other. Her red hair has become blonde, and I have become curvier with fuller breasts. Over the years we became like-minded souls, laughing at the world. We've cried together on my bed when one or both of our hearts has been shattered. We've done anything we could over the years to understand each other and the lives we live.

Sometimes we lose each other for a few months. Maybe even for several seasons. And then I'll find an eloquent postcard in my box. I'll call. We'll meet, and any time lost will be regained. Cleo and I remember the days of dancing and drink and passionate people. We have gone through life's struggles together and are pleased to find we still are the same passionate people.

FIERY

Amber Dane

Darla was the only person who caught my eye at the sex party that night. I was on vacation on the West Coast, and while I had some friends there, I didn't know the kinky scene in and out like I did back home. In a way, that freed me, and I talked to people who might not have given me the time of day in our well-worn, cliquish New York environment. Armed with the freedom of only a week's stay, I could peruse, cruise, and flirt.

I zeroed in on Darla right away. While most people had on minimal—if any—attire, much of it typical fetish gear, she was wearing what could've been underwear, or a bikini, black with bright orange flames that traced her breasts and ass, and matching platform heels, the fire shooting upward. Fire was perfect for her fiery personality—she seemed to be the kind of girl who lives her outrageousness every second, her loud laugh booming around us as we talked. She tossed her long, straight blonde hair over her shoulder, and I glimpsed the tongue ring hidden in her mouth. I leaned forward, hoping to show off my cleavage within my skin-tight red latex dress.

My eyes remained glued to her the rest of the night. I desperately wanted to play with her but had no idea if she was a top or bottom or what, and I was too much of a newbie to ask. Whenever we talked, I wiped my sweaty palms on the latex clinging to my skin and soaked in her every word. When I finally left, Mara, the friend I'd come to the party with, told me all about Darla. "She's known for being a bottom, but I've heard that sometimes, with especially pretty girls, she can be a top. I bet she'd be a wicked one, too." I pictured Darla with a whip, swinging it easily through the air with her big, muscular arms, and me lying down, taking her abuse and wanting more.

Darla and I had exchanged email addresses, but I had no great hopes for what would come of it. After all, she was an experienced local scenester, and I was a visiting wannabe. But, just my luck, Darla wrote to me the next day and said that out of all the people at the party, I was the only one she'd remotely wanted to play with. I gulped, peering closer at my laptop screen, ready to lick it in happiness. I beckoned Mara over and showed her the email—and she whistled.

I wrote back, agonizing over what to say: play it cool or show her my true feelings? I settled on, *The feeling's mutual. I'd love to play with you, especially if you're in charge. You name the time and place.* I hit SEND, shutting my eyes for luck. I'd included my number, and not an hour later, my cell phone rang. When I picked up, Darla purred, "Hey, gorgeous. How's that sweet ass of yours doing?"

A drawl I hadn't heard earlier lurked along the edges of her voice, and I shuddered at the sound. "Me and my ass are doing just fine," I replied.

"That's good to hear," she said, her words followed by a

long pause. "I'd like you to come over today," she continued. "I'd like to make your ass even finer." Her voice held all the sultry promise it had the night before. My pussy ached as she spoke, and clenched my asscheeks at the thought of submitting to her whims. I knew without a doubt that she wanted to top me, and that she'd be good at it.

"What should I wear?" I asked, deferring to her already.

"Any skirt you want, as long as there's no panties underneath." She gave me her address, and when we hung up I kicked up my heels like an extreme dork, but I didn't care.

I ran in to tell Mara, but she'd been eavesdropping in the hallway and had already figured it out. She reached over and gave my ass a squeeze. "Girl, you're in for it. You know that, right? Feel free to raid my closet if that'll help." I didn't really have time to ponder the first half of what she'd said, because I was panicking about what to wear. A short skirt or something more modest? Bra or no bra? Hair down or up? I looked at myself in the mirror to get a clue. My long brown hair was all over the place, as usual, some of it falling down my back, some spread over my shoulders. I smoothed it out, running my fingers through the soft tresses, and let the ends fall over my breasts. I was wearing a typically low-cut black top, my ample cleavage hovering in the V. I slipped out of my jeans, then turned to look at the lacy thong bisecting my ass. I was happy with what I saw, the result of solid hours at the gym, climbing my way on the Stairmaster to backdoor paradise, as much as one can at the gym.

I scoured the filled-to-the-brim racks of Mara's closet, until the perfect skirt appeared. It was soft and purple, and when I put it on, it fell over my ass perfectly, accentuating my tight curves but leaving just enough to the imagination. I paired it with a tight black tank top for contrast and a pair of tall heels. I kept the shirt, brushing my hair till it shone and skipping jewelry that might get caught on anything.

In what felt like no time at all, I was ready. After I passed Mara's quickie inspection, I was off, walking the five blocks to Darla's and growing increasingly nervous. I wasn't afraid she'd hurt me, at least not in any way I didn't want, but still, playing with a new partner, especially one as beautiful and intense as Darla, was intimidating. She had to know she had me wrapped around her little finger.

As I walked, I thought about her hands, tiny but powerful, and just what they could do to me, my pussy clenching beneath my flowing skirt the whole time. I always wear underwear, not just because I'm naturally juicy, but because I feel safer wrapped in those private sheer layers that only I know about until I choose to reveal them. I'm the kind of girl who always has a well-stocked panty drawer, even when it feels like I have nothing else to wear. At least I know my pussy's protected.

But, following Darla's instructions, I wasn't wearing panties, and from the way the skirt clung so perfectly to my ass, anyone walking behind me could tell exactly what was going on. Not that I minded, exactly. It was just a new sensation.

By the time I stood on Darla's porch ringing the doorbell, it wasn't the brisk walk that had gotten me panting. When she answered the door wearing just a red camisole and panties, I caught my breath. "Hi," I managed. The word almost caught in my throat as she took my hand and led me inside. I realized it really hadn't mattered what either of us wore; the electricity charging from her palm into mine spoke volumes more than any lacy finery. I felt the power of her attraction working its way into my body, and in the minute it took to reach her bedroom, I became even more willing to give myself over to her. She led me to her bed, which was adorned with black satin sheets.

Darla sat me down and turned toward me, her face unexpectedly serious. She took both my hands in hers, and looking deep into my eyes, said, "Hi, yourself."

"I want you," I told her, my hands warm in hers.

"You look very nice, Amber," she said. "But I want all of you, not just a small part, or even a large one. If we're going to play together, you have to give yourself to me. That means you'll trust me to know what's best for you, what your body wants, and you believe I will provide that for you as best I can. You're always in control of your actions, but I can't be my best if I feel you're truly afraid of what I'm doing. Do you understand?"

Her eyes bore into mine. I wasn't totally sure I did understand, but I nodded anyway, because the tone of her voice sent shivers all along my spine. I wanted to be the best sub she'd ever had, the girl with the prettiest and most obedient behind she'd ever seen. I knew already it wasn't going to be a long-term thing between us. This was probably par for the course for her, but I was a visitor in all senses of the word. Nevertheless, I felt at home with her soft hands and kind eyes; her sensual, muscular body that made me want to bury my face in her cleavage.

Once she had my agreement, her tone softened. "I want you to crawl across my lap," she said, beckoning me forward. I did as she urged, and when she lifted up my skirt, even though I'd been following her orders in going commando, the way she *tisked,* her tongue against the roof of her mouth, made me feel like the naughtiest girl alive.

"Well, well, well, what do we have here?" she said, running one finger along the crack of my ass. She kept it there, pressing against my puckered hole while I willed myself to stay still. Her other hand reached forward and grabbed one of my asscheeks, pinching my skin as she thoroughly took over my behind. She moved, and all of a sudden one hand was fisted in my hair, the other massaging the small of my back. She pushed up my shirt so it bared more of my backside to her, my stomach now brushing against the softness of her silky attire. As she slid a pillow under my cheek, the sensual overload was complete. Soft curves beneath, and the start of harsh smacks above, as she brought one strong palm crashing down against my ass. I moaned into the pillow, drooling a little as she tugged my hair by its roots while spanking my other cheek.

Darla's smacks held all the power I'd seen in her strong arms, but also something more. They told me she knew I got off on being so open, so vulnerable, so needy. She knew each whack didn't just sting the outer layer of my ass but made me melt deep inside, made my pussy ache for contact while yearning for even harsher smacks. She kept right on going, her blows landing all around my curved behind and farther down, along my sensitive upper thighs. I felt my cheeks turning red.

She stopped periodically to trace a line along my ass, probably a welt, the lightness of these strokes in strong contrast to the pounding force of her smacks. I'd thought she'd been giving it her all, but I quickly learned that was nothing when it came to Darla's smacks. She lifted her arm again, then brought her hand down along my sweet spot, that special gooey quadrant of my ass that, when smacked, makes me feel I've died and gone to the kinkiest heaven possible.

Darla landed a blow solidly on my right cheek, and when her hand connected with my fleshy globe, she grabbed it, balling her hand into my fiery skin and digging in, hard. The impact was magnified by my surprise, and I bit into the pillow, grateful I hadn't screamed from the sweet pain she was giving me. Soon I got lost in the heated torment, the blows and grabs and pinches and digs blurring into one orgasmic whirlwind as Darla smacked my ass silly. By the time she was done, my legs were spread as wide as could be, my skirt up around my stomach; my hard nipples poking against my bra, mashing against her thighs as I took every last one of her fiercest whacks. My eyes burned with tears of pleasure when she finally took something soft and rubbed it against my ass.

She didn't make me look at her yet, just stroked my stinging, scorched skin, bruised and blistered to perfection, before rubbing in some cream. She'd put me in such a trance I was tempted to suck my thumb and curl into a ball, but even more than that I wanted her comfort, I wanted her touch, her talent, her trigger going off inside me. I was sure that was more than clear from the way my pussy glistened with need, clenching tightly as she caressed my ass. But Darla was going to make me say it out loud, make me tell her what I wanted.

"You sure do have a gorgeous ass, Amber, and you can take a lot. I'm proud of you." Her voice was calm and gentle as she rubbed and stroked and soothed. I moaned, half into the pillow, half into the air, as her fingers wandered lower, dancing around my lips as she traced along my bikini line, her nails lightly scraping my tender inner thighs, my palest parts. She was so near, yet for all the attention she paid my pussy, she couldn't have been farther away.

She made a move to push me aside and stand up. "I'm going to slip into something more comfortable," she said, the cliché rolling drolly off her lips. I was too limp to protest and let my eyes close. When I opened them again, it was to look behind me at the hard object probing my slick opening.

I almost laughed, because Darla's idea of "comfortable" was clearly her own invention. Gone was her sexy loungewear, and in its place she wore a sparkly red harness and a bulging black cock standing proudly in front of her, a red-lipsticked smile of triumph blaring across her face. She held her new dick in front of her, poised to enter me, and without saying another word, she did just that, her lubed-up member pressing its way into my molten center. Immediately I spasmed around her sleek invasion, putting my head back on the pillow and spreading my legs as wide as possible, so they were practically perpendicular to the rest of me. She pushed deeper, until I felt the head of the dildo nudge my inner wall. My butt burned with the very recent memory of her hands, but I couldn't think about that at all because her cock rocked in and out of me, slowly but surely building me up to the point of no return.

Darla continued to have her way with me, while I could only muster enough energy to lie there and take what she offered, my body hers through and through. I was grateful we were alone, without the umpteen prying eyes of her fellow city playmates watching as I gave it up to this kinky goddess. I wasn't embarrassed, exactly, but I knew how I must have looked, my clothes shoved up but still on, my face tear-streaked, my ass bright red. Darla lived up to every promise her ravishing eyes had telegraphed at the party and more; she was a technically expert spanker with her own patented technique, exuding a personal power that let me know this meant something to her too, even if we were just onetime lovers. When she was finally done, I thought I was too, my body floundering as I recovered from her precious assault.

"Not so fast," she said when I attempted to slip away. "I think you need some more." Shedding the strap-on, she drew me back to my earlier position across her lap.

It was one thing to be splayed like that when she was spanking me; then, it made sense. But to have her fuck me in this position was almost too much. I buried my red face into her leg, embarrassed at giving away my body's secrets so easily, but Darla didn't lord it over me. In fact, she was almost tender as she slipped her warm fingers inside me—two, and then I think it was three—stroking my hair, cooing at me, the antithesis of the fierce domme she'd been earlier.

It didn't take long before I melted against her, nearly sliding off her as my orgasm shook me all the way through. She kept her fingers inside me, still and strong, long after I was done. When I tried to return the favor, wanting to somehow give her back even a fraction of the joy she'd given me, she held a finger to my lips to shush me. "You've given me more than enough to-day, Amber. Maybe next time you're in town..." It was sweet of her to say that, because we both knew it wasn't going to happen. It was the equivalent of a halfhearted, "I'll call you."

I straightened my hair and got dressed in a daze, my body electrified by what she'd done to me. I kissed her good-bye and left, lost in thought as walked back to where I was staying, knowing it'd be a while before my ass could withstand anything harder than a cushion beneath it.

Even though my thoughts were a little bittersweet on the flight back to New York, I don't know that I would have wanted to see Darla again. She's the kind of girl who sweeps into your life like a fast-moving storm, rearranging everything in its path, and just when you come to grips with what's happening, she's gone, leaving only the results of her work behind. Unlike a storm, though, her power was invisible, yet I feel it every time I see a girl with a certain gleam in her eye, the kind that transmits special signals for me. In fact, I rarely think about Darla so directly—she's usu-ally more of a passing memory, a faint twinge as I bend over for my current lover to take her smacks. But sometimes it's nice to take a trip through history, and certainly, out of all the girls I've bedded, Darla's the one who had the biggest impact, in more ways than one.

MY ORANGE VALENTINE

Aunt Fanny

I met Traf six years ago in the fantasy room at Gay.com. We started our relationship proving the existence of God to a nonbeliever in the chat room by each bringing up love. If falling in love isn't a true miracle, I don't know one. She approached it through her Catholicism. I came at it from the gestalt viewpoint of a higher being consisting of all living things in the universe. We found our commonalities, the differences being minor.

Traf and I met in March, quickly moved in together, and committed to a monogamous relationship in April. The sex was fantastic, maybe even a little too much for me. I was forty-three while Traf was fifty-two. Even so, she was in fantastic shape and enjoyed four to five hours of lovemaking at a time. I on the other hand was ecstatic after the first hour, satiated after the second, tired during the third, and in pain during the fourth. For me it was more about the quality of sex than the quantity. But I didn't complain, because just days before meeting her I'd ended a sexless two-year relationship. It seemed like feast or famine to me. I thought maybe I was out of practice.

Since then, our lives have melded together. Her children and grandchildren like me and call me Nana. Our community is friendly, and no one has a problem with two lesbians living in their neighborhood. We have a joint bank account, keep no passwords on our computers, and try hard to be honest and forthcoming with each other. We call each other *honey* and *sweetheart* and even *babe* freely, even in public. We're a traditional butch/femme couple. I wear lipstick, high heels, and jewelry. Traf wears starched button-down shirts, pleated slacks, and comfortable shoes. She supports my writing, and I support her passion for fishing. We're good for each other.

As fate would have it, my birthday falls two days before Valentine's Day. All my life up until meeting Traf, my lovers have taken advantage of this fact by buying only one present for the two occasions. Granted, it's usually a nice piece of jewelry, but still. A woman wants to feel special as a lover on Valentine's Day, not as if her birthday's being celebrated two days late.

Traf didn't wait. On the Sunday of my birthday that first year she took me out to dinner at a top-notch restaurant and gave me a gorgeous amethyst-and-gold ring. Afterward, we went out drinking and dancing into the wee hours of the morning.

Monday was the legal holiday for Abraham Lincoln's birthday, and Tuesday it was back to work for everyone in our snowbound Minnesota town. I had enjoyed immensely our evening out, but I expected that would be it.

I spent Tuesday writing. I've only had time to do it since moving in with Traf. I'm driven to write, although the rejection letters keep pouring in. When I get deep into a book or story, I forget to eat or move from my chair. Traf knows this, and that day she pulled me out once or twice just to get me to stretch and have something to eat. Then I went straight back to it, determined to get a certain chapter just right.

At six o'clock Traf appeared at my office door. She was dressed in a nice pair of blue slacks. Her breasts were constrained by the man's undershirt clearly visible through her starched white shirt. She looked good enough to eat. "Time to quit for the day," she said. "Can you wrap it up in the next five minutes?"

"Sure," I told her. I was satisfied. I still had some tweaking to do, but the basics were down, and I felt I could leave it until tomorrow. "What's for dinner?" I asked. One of the deals we have when I'm writing is that she does the meal planning and cooking, while all I have to do is the dishes. And Traf is an excellent cook.

"Al catra," she answered, making me salivate. I focused my nose and smelled the delicious aroma. Traf was born in the Azores, and the smell of the rich red-wine-soaked beef roasting in a clay pot in a slow oven made hope soar in my heart. We were having a Valentine's dinner. Al catra is not for everyday eating.

"Do I have time to shower?" I asked casually, rising from my desk. I'd expected to be treated by Traf the same way I had by all my exes. I needed a few minutes to clean up and get perfumed, coiffed, and bejeweled.

"As a matter of fact," Traf said, smiling at me, "I've already drawn you a bath." She took my hand and pulled me down the corridor. I could smell what I thought were fragrant candles burning before I saw them in the sparkling-clean bathroom. The white tile and shiny chrome gleamed under the fluorescent lights, which were still on. Dozens of roses, a rainbow of colors, sat in large vases on the counter.

The bathtub was filled with steaming-hot water, a dozen

bright oranges rolling around the bottom of it. The scent of the fruit was the fragrance I'd noticed earlier. "Like my story," I said, referring to a piece of erotica I'd written for her.

"I thought we could try it," Traf said with a big grin. "You need to relax," she added soothingly into my ear. "Enjoy your fantasy." Her nearness sparked a familiar warmth throughout my body. This was going to be fun.

"Oh, honey!" I cried happily. She turned me to face her and pushed me gently back into the doorjamb, grabbing my arms and pinning them over my head. She leaned in and kissed me.

It started softly, her lips pressing gently on mine, but then she probed with her tongue. I parted my lips and invited her in. Our tongues dueled playfully. I felt her release my hands and pull me into her body. She pinched the straps of my sleeveless dress in her thumbs and pulled them down my shoulders, her strong fingers grazing my flesh. I reached behind me and unzipped. Traf tugged on my red dress, and it slid down to my hips.

My breasts were encased in a white lace bra, the matching panties peeking above my draped dress. I'm not too large, but I'm not too small either, and my breasts have stood up well over the years. I'm proud of them and drew in a breath to make them swell. Traf growled and buried her head in my cleavage. Her fingers found and sprung my bra hooks, her hands circling quickly to claim my breasts as they swung free. I shook off the bra, more intent on her thumbs circling my nipples. She lowered her head again and sucked first one, then the other, taking her time and doing it right. I moaned.

Traf pushed my skirt and panties down until they puddled at my feet. She helped me out of them, then reached behind me to switch off the light. The room twinkled by the light of dozens of candles scattered everywhere. She took my hand and led me to the bathtub, then helped me settle to the bottom, among the rolling oranges. The warm water embraced my tired body, and I leaned back.

Our claw-foot tub is old and deep. I sank down until my shoulders were underwater, allowing the warmth to envelope me. I felt completely at ease in my world. Traf leaned over the tub and kissed me. I closed my eyes, completely content.

Ending the kiss, Traf knelt beside the tub, rolled up the sleeves of her white shirt, and reached for one of the oranges clustered on either side of me. She managed to tickle my inner thigh with it on her way up. I watched her with lazy eyes, anticipating. After all, I wrote the story. "I know what you're going to do," I murmured, with a giggle.

"You ought to," she laughed back, rising to her feet. She went to the end of the tub and reached back in the water for one of my feet. The warm orange rolled luxuriously against the arch of my foot. Thus began one of the greatest massages of all time.

That wonderful plump fruit was just firm enough to manipulate my aching muscles, and Traf's hands followed through. She spent a long while just on the base of my feet, then traveled up to my calves. It was wonderful.

She moved to the head of the tub, just behind me. The orange rolled over my neck, its warmth spreading into muscles tensed from hunkering over a laptop all day. Traf used her strength to push down on my shoulders, helping me relax further. Then she leaned me forward and worked her wondrous orange over my back. Her fingers skimmed my skin, igniting a trail of fire, but she concentrated on the massage.

Finally she leaned me back in the tub, cradling my head on a folded towel. Her massage continued along my neck, then traced my cleavage and circled my breasts. My breathing quickened, but she wasn't through yet.

Pulling her ever-present knife from her pocket, she sliced the orange neatly in two. She held each half over my breasts and squeezed.

Warm orange juice burst over my skin, trickling down my belly into the water around me. "Oh, my God," I cried.

Traf leaned over and slowly licked up the juice from first one, then the other breast. "Not quite," she laughed. She dribbled more on them and kept licking. I mixed my own fingers with the juice, the softness of my breast, and the firm insistence of her tongue. She leaned back to look at me, dropping the orange into the water and using her bare hands to massage my breasts.

"You look so handsome," I said, enjoying the play of her biceps under her sleeves. "But perhaps you need to take another bath?" I nodded, encouraging her to join me.

"I will. Oh, I will," Traf agreed enthusiastically. "Later."

"Do some of the other things in my story," I urged her. She raised her head and grinned at me. Reaching down beside my leg she extracted another orange. Taking up her knife again, she peeled it in one long strip, never removing her eyes from mine. It was impressive as hell. She took the rind and sliced it neatly into four pieces, tossing them into the water where they floated, curlicues of bright orange.

Peeling one section free, she placed it gently against my lips. "Like this?" she asked me playfully.

My lips have always been supersensitive erogenous zones. I felt them swell as I grinned, keeping them closed to continue enjoying the orange slice softly tracing their outline. They tingled and swelled even more. I flicked my tongue tip playfully at the orange. It invaded.

The firm warmth pressed through my lips to enter my mouth. Its fat flesh began to pump in and out, fucking my mouth. My tongue danced around it, anticipating, enjoying. I raked the orange slice with my teeth, appreciating the sudden burst of flavor breaking free from its tender skin. Traf held the piece still, and I bit through it, chewing softly. She pressed the other half into my mouth, then reached for another section.

This one she drew over my face, teasing my skin with it. She circled my ears, traced my nose, descended my neck, and finally circled my nipples. The piece of orange painted strokes of desire on my skin. It descended below the waterline, tracing my belly and playfully tickling my navel. It traced the outline of my deep red curls, then made a Y down the meeting of my thighs. I parted my legs eagerly.

"I love you," husked Traf as she always did before entering me. She used her fingers to hold open my two lower lips, then traced the firm fruit over my slit and clit. I moaned.

"*Querida,*" I sighed. "*Minha amante.*" I reached up my arms and encircled her neck. She kissed me at the same moment she pushed the orange slice into my pussy. I thrust my tongue into her mouth as she used her fingers to slide it in and out of me. My pussy clenched around it, squeezing.

Traf paused, pulling away from our kiss but leaving the fruit inside me. She reached into the tub and raised first one of my legs over the edge, then the other. I was spread-eagled before her hungry gaze. She reached to retrieve the orange nestled within me. She brought it to her lips and held my gaze as she bit into it, chewing it slowly.

Scooping up another orange from the bottom of the tub, she brought it to my nose. The pungent aroma stimulated me. The smell of orange peel has always heightened my self-awareness. The room was now swimming in it.

"Watch me peel this," Traf commanded softly. I opened my eyes to find her warm brown ones soft with love. I shifted my gaze to her hands, cradling the fruit as she often did my face. She raised it to her mouth and ripped through the thick skin with sharp white teeth. Petal-shaped bits of orange rind began to fill the water around me as she tore and dropped each piece. She kept biting until the orange was naked, then pulled it in half, scooping away the pulpy rind in the center. I watched as her long talented tongue found a nub at one end and began persistently licking it. She nibbled it with her lips then traced her tongue along the center of the fruit, to find and circle the nub once more. She pressed at it.

I touched my clit in the water, knowing she could see exactly what I was doing. "Oh, yeah, baby," she paused to say. Then her tongue began to mimic the action of my busy fingers on the orange nub once more.

I reached up with my free hand and grabbed the orange from her. I dropped it in the water with the others and tugged at her shirt. I wanted her in the tub with me, now. "Get in here, lover," I said huskily.

"Yes, ma'am." She grinned wickedly, brown eyes sparkling in the candlelight.

Traf stood up and quickly removed her clothes. When she got down to her boxers she began to dance for me, her breasts swaying against her chest. She tugged playfully on first one side then the other, always dancing just out of my reach when I'd try to help. Finally she turned her back and dropped her drawers.

I love her ass. It's high and round, firm and plump. She shook it at me, then turned and climbed in the opposite end of the tub. Her feet settled firmly against my pussy, my legs still spread wide over the edges of the tub. One big toe settled firmly on my clit, shoving my fingers aside. Traf used her talented toe to stimulate me. She reached for one of the peeled oranges rolling around us, and pulled off a section two slices wide. I grinned at her.

"You wouldn't!" I challenged playfully.

"I would," she disagreed with an evil grin, and proved it by pushing the section into my spread pussy. I arched my back at the feeling inside me. Traf tore free another section and pushed it into me as well. I moaned in excitement. A third section filled me. A fourth started to slip back out. She pushed it in. It slid out again. She pushed. I started to shake as the pressure began to build inside me. Traf pulled her toe away from my clit, and I subsided. Then she palmed my pussy and put her thumb where her toe had been. I closed my eyes and moaned.

The warm water laced with orange oil sluiced over my breasts and shoulders as I rode her hand. With every sway of my hips she pushed the orange wedges deep within me over and over again. Her mouth descended on a nipple, still sticky with orange juice. She sucked me, teasing the tip with her tongue. As my first orgasm started, her thumb quickened its pace. I shuddered on her hand and into her mouth. "*Querida*," she murmured as my body quieted.

She gathered me up in her arms, switching us around until she cradled my body between her spread legs. I was fulfilled, satiated, totally relaxed. There was no better place to be in this world than within the sheltered cove of her body. I sighed, nestling into her neck. She bent down and kissed me.

I love the feeling of her breasts against my back. I rubbed my shoulder blades into them, relishing the feel of them. Her dark nipples hardened against my skin. Traf's large hands cupped my breasts, and as she pulled them back, I floated against her own.

She palmed my nipples, as hers pushed sharply into my back. I pushed my bottom down against her pussy, swaying gently to urge her lower lips open. I started to turn in the water.

"Wait," said Traf, with a smile. "There's something I need to do first." She pulled me up onto my knees in the water, so that my bottom faced her. She used one hand to bend me forward, while the other one pulled back my hips. She fastened her mouth to my pussy and sucked.

One by one the sections of orange were sucked from my pussy. Each time, Traf took the time to chew it, nuzzling my ass and kissing it, or taking the occasional swipe at my clit with her tongue. I loved being exposed to her this way, feeling her hands and lips caress me. By the time she'd checked my pussy thoroughly with her tongue to be sure it was clear, I was ready for round two. I turned and sank back into the water, facing her.

I reached between her legs and found an untouched orange. I drew it up across her dark brown triangle, and over her belly. Then, using her knife, I inexpertly sliced it in half. I tore the pulpy fiber from its center. Then I fit each half directly over Traf's nipples. I rubbed them gently, knowing her nipples were jumping to attention. I squeezed.

The pulp of the orange exploded under the pressure of my fingers, and I mashed the fruit into my lover's breasts. When my fingers met her skin I massaged her deeply, squishing the orange against her. Then I bent to lick her clean.

I love Traf's breasts. They're round and full, swaying gently against her rib cage. Her nipples are perfect, a rich deep brown. I filled my hands with them, tracing my tongue across her hot skin. I took my time, enjoying what I was doing too much to hurry. Traf finally wrapped my hair in her hands, cupped my face, and pulled me up her naked body for a kiss.

Her breasts teased mine, our bellies flat against each other. My pussy rode hers, and I slipped my legs between her thighs to further the contact. I pushed against her, rubbing in tiny circles until I'd freed her clit. My own was throbbing when they touched, and the dance they did together lit a fire in both our bellies. We love to clit-fuck.

I rode her until her breath came quickly, her breasts rising and falling against mine. Then I pulled back.

"Go get your cock," I commanded. She grinned at me wolfishly then rose and stepped out of the tub. I admired the view of her ass disappearing out of the bathroom, then turned my attention to releasing the cool water around me and refilling the tub with hot. Traf loves hot, hot water.

She stepped back into the tub, fully strapped and at attention. My eyes filled with passion for my handsome butch. I stopped her while she was still on her knees, and hoisted myself into the same position. I held the last unpeeled orange in my hand and brought it to her lips. "Bite it," I ordered.

She did as I said, then watched with fascination as I tore away the rest of the peel. I held the orange up before her eyes, and used one thumb to widen the opening at one end. I teased the hole with my thumb, the bright red of my nail polish against the white-lace-covered orange. Traf's eyes followed every movement.

I upended the orange and plunged it down over the head of her cock. She gasped. The special cup at its end was filled with rubber nubs, and as one touched her engorged clit, she arched her back. She quickly looked back down to watch as I moved the orange up and down over her cock.

I held it in both hands, but I quickly released one to reach between her legs. Two of my fingers entered her as my thumb pressed under the cup to find and circle her clit. I kept both hands pumping in the same rhythm, and Traf gasped as I leaned forward and captured one nipple with my lips. I sucked it in.

I raked her nipple with the tip of my teeth, teasing it with my tongue. My fingers in her pussy felt the walls contract. My fist pumping the orange up and down on her cock caused it to rock into my other hand, crushing my thumb against her clit and pushing my fingers ever deeper. Hot water swirled her thighs as they clenched around my hand, trapping it in place.

Traf rocked her hips, fucking the orange with her cock. My lips traveled up her neck, biting and kissing until I'd captured her earlobe. I blew gently.

Shivers spread from her center as she started to come. I pressed hard with the orange and swirled her clit firmly with my thumb. I sent a third finger inside her, and she rocked up and down on me. Her breasts bounced before my eyes.

She sank her ass against the edge of the tub, and I kept my hands busy as she slammed through one orgasm after another. I encouraged each aftershock into yet another climax. She finally seized both of my hands with her own, effectively stopping me. "Don't," she begged. "It's too much." I smiled at her tenderly as I removed my hands, dropping the orange into the tub.

We nestled into the water, wrapped in each other's arms. I think I even fell asleep on her shoulder for a moment. When we rose, we took turns tenderly toweling each other dry.

I brought us clean robes, and we wore them to dinner. My amethyst ring glimmered in the light of the candles Traf had brought from the bathroom. She gave me a small box containing matching earrings. The al catra was beyond delicious, boiled potatoes soaking up the fabulous au jus. Rich red wine filled fine glass stemware. Our finest china graced the table. In the background, k.d. sang softly from the stereo.

We did the dishes together, Traf's soapy hands massaging mine in the water. She brushed against me when passing to put things away. I knew from experience that she was far from satisfied. Although I was tired from my long day of writing and fantastic sex, I knew there would be more.

We went to the bedroom, pulled off our robes, and climbed into our queen-size bed to warm ourselves under the thick blankets. I turned into Traf's arms, expecting another round, probably followed by another bout. My lover surprised me by turning me over and spooning against my naked back, satisfied to hold me in her arms. She nuzzled the nape of my neck and whispered into my ear, "We'll have plenty of time for lovemaking in the years to come." She cupped my breast in her hand the way she does every night while we fall asleep. "Happy Valentine's Day, beloved."

"Happy Valentine's Day, *minha amante*," I murmured. I was happier than I'd ever been. I loved this woman more than anyone in my life and knew beyond any doubt that there is a God.

We snuggled for a while, and as I drifted off to sleep she whispered in my ear, "You're a really great writer. You could make it big one day. You should publish that story." I smiled to myself, thoroughly in love with my muse. My beloved. My orange valentine.

ABOUT THE EDITOR

CHELSEA JAMES lives in Brooklyn, N.Y., where she writes and edits all kinds of naughty stories. She's currently working on *Her Skin*, a deliciously dirty novel. *After Midnight* is her first anthology, but she has many more in the pipeline.

Classic Sex Guides

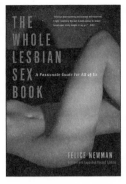

**Buy 4 books,
Get 1 FREE***

The Whole Lesbian Sex Book
A Passionate Guide For All of Us
Second Edition
Felice Newman
ISBN 1-57344-199-6 $24.95

"Infectious and empowering and extremely well researched. I highly recommend this book to every woman: bi, lesbian, almost queer, totally straight, or boy-girl. Getting off is good, and this book will help you get off better." —*Bust*

"Sets a standard for which all popular sex writers should aim. Not just for lesbians—heterosexual women could learn a great deal about themselves." —*Library Journal*

The Good Vibrations Guide to Sex
The Most Complete Sex Manual Ever Written
Third Edition
Cathy Winks and Anne Semans
Illustrated by Phoebe Gloeckner
"Useful for absolutely everyone. Old, young, fit, disabled, gay, straight, or working out the details, this book tells you, shows you, and reassures you."
—*O, The Oprah Magazine*
ISBN 1-57344-158-9 $25.95

**The Ultimate Guide
to Anal Sex for Women**
Tristan Taormino
Expanded and Updated Second Edition
Recommended by the *Playboy* Advisor and *Loveline*—the only sex guide on anal sex for women. "A book that's long overdue!...informative, sexy, and inspirational."
—Betty Dodson
ISBN 1-57344-221-6 $16.95

The Ultimate Guide to Cunnilingus
How to Go Down on a Woman and Give Her Exquisite Pleasure
Violet Blue
"One heck of a crash course."
—*East Bay Express*
ISBN 1-57344-144-9 $14.95

The Ultimate Guide to Strap-On Sex
A Complete Resource for Women & Men
Karlyn Lotney (a.k.a. Fairy Butch)
The complete guide to dildos and harnesses—for everyone interested in strap-on play—women and men of all sexual orientations and genders.
ISBN 1-57344-085-X $14.95

Sensuous Magic
A Guide to S/M for Adventurous Couples
Second Edition
Patrick Califia
For all couples interested in exploring bondage, S/M, dominance and submission—women and men of all sexual orientations
ISBN 1-57344-130-9 $14.95

---

* Free book of equal or lesser value. Shipping and applicable sales tax extra.
Cleis Press • (800) 780-2279 • orders@cleispress.com
www.cleispress.com

Best Erotica Series

"Gets racier every year."—*San Francisco Bay Guardian*

Best of Best Women's Erotica
Edited by Marcy Sheiner
ISBN 1-57344-211-9 $14.95

Best Women's Erotica 2006
Edited by Violet Blue
ISBN 1-57344-223-2 $14.95

Best Women's Erotica 2005
Edited by Marcy Sheiner
ISBN 1-57344-201-1 $14.95

Best Women's Erotica
Edited by Marcy Sheiner
ISBN 1-57344-099-X $14.95

Best Black Women's Erotica
Edited by Blanche Richardson
ISBN 1-57344-106-6 $14.95

Best Black Women's Erotica 2
Edited by Samiya Bashir
ISBN 1-57344-163-5 $14.95

Best Bisexual Women's Erotica
Edited by Cara Bruce
ISBN 1-57344-134-1 $14.95

Best Fetish Erotica
Edited by Cara Bruce
ISBN 1-57344-146-5 $14.95

Best of Best Lesbian Erotica 2
Edited by Tristan Taormino
ISBN 1-57344-212-7 $14.95

Best of the Best Lesbian Erotica: 1996-2000
Edited by Tristan Taormino
ISBN 1-57344-105-8 $15.95

Best Lesbian Erotica 2006
Edited by Tristan Taormino
Selected and Introduced by Eileen Myles
ISBN 1-57344-224-0 $14.95

Best Lesbian Erotica 2005
Edited by Tristan Taormino. Selected
and Introduced by Felice Newman
ISBN 1-57344-202-X $14.95

Best of Best Gay Erotica 2
Edited by Richard Labonté
ISBN 1-57344-213-5 $14.95

Best of the Best Gay Erotica: 1996-2000
Edited by Richard Labonté
ISBN 1-57344-104-X $14.95

Lips Like Sugar
Women's Erotic Fantasies
Edited by Violet Blue
ISBN 1-57344-232-1 $14.95

Hot Lesbian Erotica
Edited by Tristan Taormino
ISBN 1-57344-208-9 $14.95

**Buy 4 books,
Get 1 FREE***

Ordering is easy! Call us toll free to place your MC/VISA order or mail the order form below with payment to: Cleis Press, P.O. Box 14697, San Francisco, CA 94114.

ORDER FORM

Buy 4 books, Get 1 FREE*

QTY	TITLE	PRICE
____	_____	_____
____	_____	_____
____	_____	_____
____	_____	_____
____	_____	_____
____	_____	_____
____	_____	_____
____	_____	_____
____	_____	_____
____	_____	_____

SUBTOTAL _____

SHIPPING _____

SALES TAX _____

TOTAL _____

Add $3.95 postage/handling for the first book ordered and $1.00 for each additional book. Outside North America, please contact us for shipping rates. California residents add 8.5% sales tax. Payment in U.S. dollars only.

* Free book of equal or lesser value. Shipping and applicable sales tax extra.
Cleis Press • (800) 780-2279 • orders@cleispress.com
www.cleispress.com
You'll find more great books on our website